PRAISE FOR *ANGEL TRACKS*

"What a story. I was hooked from the beginning. The emotional devastation that Pat experienced comes through loud and clear. Debbie's character is portrayed beautifully, and some of her spirit seems to eke from the pages. Pat's message of healing is quite profound, and gifts the reader with a real sense of hope."
~Peggy Stautberg, Editor, The Book Connection, Houston, Texas

"I told Pat I was a slow reader but couldn't put this down and read it in one sitting. Pat pours the deepest parts of her heart into her writings. She has a far-reaching faith in God and an undying love for her daughter and mom."
~Beverly Peyton, Teacher, Jersey Village Baptist church, Jersey Village, Texas

Angel Tracks

Pat Morgan

ISBN: 978-0-9850066-5-5

Library of Congress Control Number: 2012937513

Cover Design by All Things That Matter Press

Published in 2012 by All Things That Matter Press

TO DEBBIE
and
THE BIG FIVE

Foreword

One day in July, 2007, I was in my study writing a new short play; a quick ten minute job for a contest submission. It was a play about penguins finding true love. An Oscar Madison meets *The Flying Nun* sort of thing. My latest short play had just placed in the annual Scriptwriters/Houston 10 x 10 Competition and the cast was rehearsing once a week on my back porch. The play was opening August 17th and we were hard at work under three fans and a stocked cooler. *Capote Tonight*, my full-length had just closed in Houston at Express Theatre that past May after a three week run, starring Paul Young as the memorable Truman Capote. Our audiences loved Paul's Truman and jammed the lobby after every performance to meet our flamboyant star. In short, my life on the boards was kickin' ass.

Anyway, that hot Houston afternoon, while working away in my Alpha state of coma where I write from, there but mostly not, a dark shadow slowly moved across my left peripheral vision. Now I have two black lab mix dogs that wander into my study from time to time looking for attention, a nap under the fan, or a cookie. Thinking one of them had invited himself in I reached my hand down to give him a greeting pet. Not there. I made a couple passes at him but no hairy head. Raising my consciousness up a notch, I turned to the left to see where the dog had gotten himself and no dog. Not beside me, not up on the day bed, or under the desk, and by then the black shadow had faded.

Having read somewhere that the body can react to something before the mind can process it, I broke into a cold sweat as goose bumps the size of eggs beat a path down my arms. Hairs rose over my entire body and I shivered as the bristles on the back of my neck stood straight up.

Slowly looking about the room, my body and heartbeat gradually returned to normal and I thankfully acknowledged I was not going to stroke out. Now, if you knew me, you'd know that I'm about as spooky as Yogi Bear, unless you want to count my daughter, Debbie, my mom, and I having our tarot cards read each Mother's Day for kicks. However, this incident sure had my attention and it stuck with me throughout the day. Later that evening I called Debs. We talked on an average of two to three times a week and spent at least one weekend a month together. My ninety-one year old mother lives with me and suffers from Alzheimer's. So it was much easier for Debbie to come home then for me to pack up Mom, all the pills, lotions, and blood pressure equipment that travel involved. Then there were the dogs, Casey and Duke. I had to pack up their dog food, toys, cookies, and blanket, and it all had to make the one hundred eighty mile trip to Waco. Therefore, Debbie and I talked on the phone a lot. Mom was turning ninety-two October 29th and we were beginning to plan a birthday party for her.

Debbie had never married and as she was a psychologist with the Texas Youth Commission counseling drugs and alcohol abuse, often said she had enough kid problems during the day and needed peace and quiet at night. So no grandma duties for me, but with Mom and two horse dogs to care for, it wasn't a total hardship.

Now, this kid of mine had a hobby: holistic bug-a-boos. She was into tarot cards, palmistry, angel therapy, healing and crystals. If she wasn't unsuccessfully trying to read my palm, with an instruction book in her hand, she was hauling out one of her angel kits, gleefully throwing her dice to enlighten me as to my future in theater. A future, I might add, that was as shaky as her palm reading. Not having a whole lot of patience or interest in that stuff, I passed it off as just a bit of frivolous fun. I'd have rather talked about the latest Tony winners while she and her cousin, Pam, were great fans of Shirley MacLaine and whatever channeler was currently selling a book or had filmed a reality show.

What a trooper. She never missed an opening night and if I needed her help with Grandma, or like the year before when I had my back surgery, she was there running everything like a Marine sergeant before I could hang up the phone. So who was I going to I tell about this "black shadow" business? Debbie.

"Hi, it's mom." As if she didn't know.

"What's going on? How's Grams?"

"Fine," I said, "except for having five of her bras in the wash today and I did the laundry yesterday. Listen, no sense in you coming home this weekend we'll be rehearsing *Sex Games* Saturday and Sunday afternoon. I'm feeding actors all weekend. It's the least I can do with what community theater pays them."

Feeding actors is not as hard as you may think. They eat anything because they're always hungry. Most work two and three part-time jobs, grab food on the fly, and are eternally grateful for a meal at six p.m. after a day of bussing dishes or foaming lattes.

I could hear a crunch. "What are you eating?"

"An apple. I just got in. Have you killed the director yet?"

"No, but close. She's as crazy as a loon. Last week one of the actors questioned her about something and she said, "No, we're not doing it that way." "But it's in the script," he wailed. "Oh, don't worry about that," she answered, "it's not important." Like the author wasn't sitting right there. We all just looked at each other.

"How's work?" I asked.

"One of my kids decided it would be a super idea to take out a ceiling tile and crawl up there in the rafters so we'd think he ran off." Running off was a common activity at the Texas Youth Commission.

"What'd you have to do, crawl up there and get him out?" No easy task as Debbie is a big girl.

"Shit, mom, it must have been a hundred ten degrees up there. He came out himself, crying, dehydrated and carrying his balls. He's in Waco with the sheriff thinking it over."

"Nice," I said, then got to it. "Listen, something happened here at the house today that should interest you."

"Yeah?"

I could tell she thought I was going to go off on her grandmother so I quickly told her my story.

"It wasn't so much the dark shadow," I concluded. "It was my body's reaction to it. Jesus, it took me half an hour and a glass of chardonnay to calm down."

She started to laugh. "Well," she said, "you had one."

"One what?" I asked.

"A visitation."

"Are we talking about some sort of ghost garbage here?"

"Naaaa," she answered. "It was probably a friendly spirit or maybe an angel just saying hello."

"Well," I said, "tell it to stay the hell out of my study. It scared the crap out of me."

And so it began.

One: Just a Little Germ

Houstonians have only two goals during August: stay cool and survive another summer. Summer comes on quickly. March and April escort a lovely, cool, blooming spring into the Bayou City. The evenings reflect blazing sunsets; and as the night air chills, azaleas and night blooming jasmine bud. You can crank open a bedroom window, pull a comforter up to your ears, and sleep a deep, dark sleep, feeling the soft breeze that gently lifts a lace curtain and makes the dogs twitch their ears. Your last thought before slipping under is hoping the gardenias will soon bloom. In the morning you can hear the doves cooing in the pear tree planning their day.

The first week in August, 2007, was pretty normal, at least normal for me. Tuesday, Mom and I traveled to the dentist, on Saturday a movie, and on Sunday our indulgence, a matinee performance play. My play, *Sex Games*, was still in rehearsal on my back porch. Fans and cold drinks were running full throttle. I made light suppers and offered up outrageously fattening desserts every week because you can always count on actors being starved *and* talented. And, if they're full of sugar, absolutely charming. This was the final week of rehearsals as hell week began the following Monday. That's when it all comes together. Setting lights, stacking programs, finishing sets, arranging props, final blocking on stage, while coordinating music cues and sound effects.

We were down to the wire. Mom and I had haircuts, manicures, pedicures, and purchased wine as cast and crew gifts, besides nursing frayed nerves. Debbie was coming home that next weekend because she had to work the weekend of August 17th when the show opened. This would be one of the few openings she missed. Usually she took off work early on Friday and drove to Houston for the event. We always made it a big deal an early movie, dinner, and then off to the theater for opening night. She loved it all. After all, this was her mom, the playwright. There was all the excitement and recognition for a mother that suffered from an inferiority complex as big as the Grand Canyon. I was convinced that someone would stalk down the center aisle, ask if I wrote this lame play, grab me by the scruff of the neck, and throw me into the street. But Debbie couldn't come home this time. Half of my support group would not be there. TYC, the Texas Youth Commission, was in the middle of an extensive investigation regarding child abuse. Austin was tearing into everything in order to satisfy the media that all was being done to investigate these state-wide charges at every TYC facility and correct them. The Mart Correctional School was under federal siege, and Debbie had more on her mind than a play. The state was closing some correctional facilities and moving kids to new locations. Mart was to receive about two hundred additional kids, and dorms had to be cleaned and prepared for their arrival on September 1st.

Mart is about one hundred eighty miles north of Houston and a straight shot up I-45 heading for Dallas. You pass Lake Conroe and Lake Livingston, both man-made lakes, and shoot into Huntsville which houses Huntsville State University, which was Debbie's alma mater, and the State of Texas' maximum security prison. You're deep in the piney woods now, and you can't imagine who started the rumor that Texas was flat. Pine trees tower above the highway on both sides and hide the university from sight but the razor wire-topped fenced yards of various prison buildings, complete with parked patrol cars gives you pause. You pass through Madisonville, then Centerville, and note the landscape has changed. Gone are the stately pines as the countryside has flattened out to patches of walnut brown scrub as you pass working ranches and a battered, long silent, hamburger joint standing lonely on the side of the road. You exit at Buffalo, hang a right on Highway 164 and note the sign: WACO fifty miles. You are now in Central Texas.

Mart makes the City of Cut and Shoot, Texas, look like Las Vegas. There is no doctor, dentist, or drug store; life's basics. What it does have is Clyde's Grocery that carries everything from bluing for your last rinse, we're talking washing clothes here like wash tubs and wringer washers: ask your grandmother, to frozen Sushi, and starch in a box. Mart can also boast two gas stations, a Dairy Queen, a Family Dollar Store, a few large stone churches of various denominations, and Direct TV, as the local cable consists of Waco and Temple news, local farm and weather reports, and Gilligan Island reruns. If you wanted to see a recent movie on TV this side of Waco, you have to subscribe to both, which you do to preserve your sanity. Mart also has a movie rental establishment set up in an old store front, a café with blue booths and terrazzo floors which is always under new management. There's a defunct donut shop and lovely, gracious, friendly people, who in the fall go crazy on Friday nights supporting their local football team.

Now, this may seem quaint to some folks but driving fifty miles round trip to Waco just to get a prescription filled is, to us city folks, horrific. In short, if you're going to get sick, do it on a weekday afternoon while you're in Waco shopping because by the time you drive in from Mart to a doctor and then get a prescription filled, you could be not of this world. So the whole population of Mart, Texas, seems to migrate to Waco on Saturday or Sunday to get haircuts, streaking, pedicures, shopping, a movie, lunch out, a book at Barnes and Noble, and enough civilization to last until the next weekend.

So why did Debbie live on this windswept prairie? There were two reasons. First, she had found a really cute, little two bedroom house that came with a terrific landlord and was located five blocks from her job, and, since she was on-call most of the time it was easier to drive to Waco Saturday or Sunday, sometimes both, for life's necessities and live close to work. And that's what she did. Armed with air purifiers and nasal sprays for her dust allergy, she fought dirt streets, front and side, and a daily twenty to thirty mile an hour breeze. The second reason; she loved her job, she loved those monster kids, she loved her co-workers as family, and they loved her. The halls rang with her laughter and good cheer. She was always organizing something: a margarita night in Waco, a bagged lunch under the huge tree in her yard, a birthday party or family reunion. Her little red Charger was seen all over town as she rushed on her lunch hour to buy favors for a kid's release or arrange a retirement lunch. She knew everyone in the TYC system and they knew her. It was a town unto itself, and employees drove one hundred fifty miles to work there, many staying over a night or two with her until they got settled. Mart residents kind of stay to themselves but it was common for her to get an, "Oh, I know you. You work on over at the school."

On the evening of Tuesday, August 7th I called her and she sounded congested. She'd been to see her regular doctor, Dr. Aldridge, and he treated her for bronchitis, again with the allergies. A simple cold would slip into bronchitis very quickly and she went into a round of antibiotics and sometimes steroids to knock it out. Her weight was not a help, and her breathing, at times, was labored.

"My temp got up to one hundred and one degrees and they sent me home and to the doctor," she told me.

"Is it still up there?"

"No, it's going down. I'll probably go back to work in a day or so."

Debbie worked so much overtime that she had months of comp and sick time accumulated, so being off sick for a few days was no problem.

Wednesday evening Mom and I went to an open house. It was at Pat Silver's home, who is managing director of Express Theatre, where my *Capote Tonight* was staged the preceding May. It was an appreciation party for cast and crews of the 2006-2007 season. Her house is low and roomy with oak floors and Italian tile. Two sets of French doors lead you out to a Mexican tiled patio where glowing white iron furniture with bright colored cushions are scattered about. I wanted to go home and burn my house down.

Thursday, Debbie was still home in Mart with a slight fever and I was in Houston, uneasily cleaning house. That evening Mom and I attended The Humble Opry in Humble, Texas. We went on a bus with an AARP group and I couldn't get home fast enough. I was uneasy.

On Friday, August 10th Debbie called. Her temperature was now one hundred and two degrees. She was a sick kid. She struggled back to Dr. Aldridge in the afternoon. He was about to change her prescription when she said to him, "What's this thing on my hip? Is that a spider bite?" It looked like a boil and was red hot, the skin around it hard and feverish.

"Nope," he answered. "That's a staph infection. I'm going to lance it and clean it out. Where'd you pick this up?"

"At work, I guess. I've been helping to clean dorms for those new kids coming in. I had on rubber gloves but I kept running my hands around my elastic waist because I had a heat rash. It was hot in there."

Mom and I packed up the dogs and drove to Mart for the weekend and maybe a few days more.

Sunday morning her temperature was normal. I had changed her bandage a couple of times and it seemed to be draining well. She was up, dressed, and poking around the kitchen while I straightened up the place, did some laundry, and went to the store. I had two tickets to the new *Tuna Does Vegas* at The Grand Theatre, in Galveston, for that afternoon and called everyone I could think of to give the tickets away, but no use. It was last minute and everyone called was either busy or not wanting to drive from Houston to Galveston. Long ways, sixty miles? Come on. A five hundred mile trip in Texas is "just down the road a piece."

"I'll be fine, Mom. Go on back and see the show. After all, sixty bucks is sixty bucks. I'll probably be going back to work by Tuesday."

Reluctantly, I drove back to Houston, dropped off the dogs, and then headed for Galveston, making the show with fifteen minutes to spare, It was wonderful and the best *Tuna* ever. When we got home, I called her and she cheerfully answered. I told her about the show and asked her how she felt.

"Good. Temperature still normal," she replied.

Volunteering for refreshment detail for all four 10 x 10 performances of *Sex Games*, I'd promised to provide all the paper products. I went to Wal-Mart and loaded up my car trunk with cups, plates, napkins, toothpicks, tablecloths, et cetera, all to be used for intermission refreshments. I could hardly get the lid closed.

Monday, August 13th was the start of hell week with frantic rehearsals, a tech rehearsal on Wednesday, and a dress on Thursday. Was I preoccupied? You bet I was. Then Debbie called.

"Mom, my temperature is back up to a hundred and two degrees. I'm really sick." And she sounded it. This fever is wearing her down, I thought. "I have a four o'clock appointment at the doctor," she said.

"Call me as soon as you get out and I'll leave for Mart." I emptied the trunk, threw a few things into a small bag, grabbed dog food, leashes, and medications for Mom, and asked her to put a few changes of clothes of her own into the bag. It was four-thirty in the afternoon when she called. Dr. Aldridge had taken one look at her now fully infected hip and called the George Hartwell General Hospital. He made arrangements for a surgeon to meet her at the hospital as the infection was rapidly spreading and she needed to be opened up and cleaned out. This was "Super Bug" but we didn't know it then.

Throwing everything in the car we took off to fight Houston's five o'clock traffic. In Waco, Debbie drove herself to the hospital and checked herself in knowing Mom, Grams, and the dogs were again on their way.

Two: Who Are Those Guys?

Arriving in Mart at seven p.m., I dropped off the dogs at Debbie's house. Debbie had made arrangements for her neighbor and landlord, Alice and Sam Grueneich, to watch for me and for Alice to drive us to the Hartwell General Hospital, in Waco. After Debbie made these arrangements she gave Alice her room number, placed a small angel medallion that she kept in her car on the nightstand, and at five p.m. went into surgery, cheerful and confident.

Alice Grueneich is a pretty, well-made blonde in her fifties, and a Central Texas dynamo. She and her husband, Sam, buy up Mart homesteads, and side-by-side fix them up and either rent or sell them off at a profit. Sam works full-time in Waco at an industrial plant. He's a very large man with a round, winning face, who is quite at home in his overalls building cupboards in his workshop or riding his mower over his rental properties.

Alice, however, suits up every morning and heads for the Water Department as a part-time assistant to somebody or other. They both know exactly what's happening in Mart and what time it happened. They're both warm, loving, people, who had adopted Debbie the day she moved in. The three of them were always dabbling in something like a family reunion or a sand pile for the Grueneich grandkids. Once, Sam hauled home a huge city park swing set and set it up on the empty lot next door to Debbie's house and all the kids in the neighborhood played on it. It was a big corner lot so there was plenty of room for the swing, kids, and the on-going baseball game. We'd sit under Debbie's big tree, tending a grill while watching the games. Alice was waiting for me and we headed for the hospital.

The George Hartwell General Hospital was a fairly new facility and Debbie was put into the new wing. The room was spacious, with warm pastel colors on the walls and bright, colorful drapes. It was homey and smelled fresh, not like a hospital at all. The cafeteria had cheerful cloth tablecloths and real flowers on each table. Everything was spotlessly clean, the food hot, and the coffee strong.

Debbie's surgery was over and she was back in her room when we arrived around eight p.m. She was sitting up in bed, talking and laughing at a conversation she was having on her cell phone while sucking on a popsicle.

"Hi, Mom."

"Wow, you look like you've been on a picnic. You look great."

She hung up the phone. "Everything is good," she replied. "I was just talking to Miss Yates, at work, and she's taking care of the insurance stuff. One of the girls called and she's stopping by after work on her way home. She lives here in Waco. No such thing as visiting hours around here."

I noticed gloved nurses were busy bustling in and out. Debbie was hooked up to oxygen and had multiple IV's inserted into her neck. The nurse told me she was receiving several antibiotics and it was a better line going through the neck. She also had leggings on that kept going off with a buzz.

"What's that noise?"

"My leggings." She showed me. "They're to prevent blood clots." Fine by me.

Then Dr. Yeager entered and the popsicle melted.

"Mrs. Levy?" I nodded, not bothering to correct him. "We have a few problems here. Due to the fact that Debbie was treated for bronchitis this week and was prescribed antibiotics, these same antibiotics are messing up her blood samples and we're not getting a good reading on just what's going on here.

"Which means?" I stammered.

"The lab is having trouble identifying the bacteria. There may be more than one. I've called in an infectious disease specialist and he'll be here in the morning. Meanwhile, this thing is spreading at an alarming rate although we're pumping her full of antibiotics. There are more abscesses. I have to go in again tomorrow morning, make the incision larger and clean out all the infection I can. By then we'll know what we're dealing with and can treat her with antibiotics that will knock this out. It's just a matter of identification and the right combination of medication."

I looked over at Debbie and she looked back at me, stricken.

"I'll just have the papers brought in and get everything set up. Okay?"

"Sure." Debbie answered, looking unsure. Later she signed the papers.

"Don't you worry about one thing," I said to her. "We're right here with you. We'll be with you when you wake up and for as long as you need us. Okay?"

"Okay." Then she smiled and looked as if she really was okay with it.

Her friend from work walked in right then and they started visiting about the job and friends. Grandma and I said goodnight and told her that since she had company we'd go on back to the house but we'd be back first thing in the morning. She was also given something to help her sleep and been told she could have nothing to eat or drink after midnight. So Debbie, being the enterprising character she was, requested her visitor bring her a cheeseburger, fries, and a large diet Coke. They were happily eating and laughing together when I left to take Grandma back to Mart. We had two dogs there that had to take a leak.

When we got back to the house, I soon realized that I hadn't brought enough medication, clothes, and whatever for an extended stay. Unpacking, I asked Mom, "Where are your clothes?" I got my standard answer. "I don't know."

Muttering, I quickly walked and fed the dogs, e-mailed everyone I knew what was going on and that I would not be back in Houston for awhile. I would miss the opening and the show would have to go on without me, as well as the paper goods which were, at that moment, stacked on my garage floor. I also called Debbie's dad in Rochester, New York, and told him what I knew, although Debbie had already talked to him. No, there was no need for him to come yet.

I can't even say I was overly concerned at that point. Debbie was a strong, healthy woman, and I knew we would be over this soon and everything would be back to normal.

We were back at the hospital at eight a.m. Dr. Yeager was there.

"We've got three different bacteria working here," he said. "She's going to have a big incision but we're prepared for that. I won't be closing her up right now so we can keep her as clean as possible while we find the right antibiotic combination."

"How long will this surgery take?"

"About three hours." Then he left to go about his business. The room got busy and soon a gurney came for Debbie. It was about nine a.m. and there was no way I was going to pace that room until noon. What was going on in Mom's mind? She looked calm and did exactly what I asked of her without comment. It was the look in her eyes that gave her away; pure panic.

My white-haired, ninety pound confused mother continued to be very quiet. I didn't know exactly what she understood about Debbie's illness but she knew Debbie was sick and in the hospital. Debbie was her only grandchild and her whole life. She liked me, I guess, but Debbie hung her moon. Mother had worked hard all her life. After Dad died, she moved to a retirement village in Florida and was very active in all their activities. She filled both my and Debbie's home with crafts, made endless quilts until we were half nuts trying to find places for it all. She traveled, went to Europe twice with one of her senior groups, and then up and bought herself a travel trailer. There she was gassing it up and following the caravan of retired RV fanatics to their next destination. She drove, set it up, and was the first to cough up a basket of blueberry muffins.

She came to live with me when she was eighty. She had long since sold the RV, was starting to have trouble balancing her checkbook and remembering things. Besides, she was as mad as a hornet that all of her old friends were dying off or selling out and going to live up North with their children. Then, all of a sudden, it was her turn.

While Debbie was in surgery, mom and I drove to Sears at a nearby mall to pick up a few clothes for her, had haircuts, and a grabbed quick lunch. We were better walking and doing something, trying to put what was going on back at the hospital out of our minds. We were back at the hospital at noon waiting. At two p.m., down Debbie came. She was awake as we met the gurney in the hall. She was talking to me and her grandmother when she began to cry.

"Are you in pain?" asked one of her nurses.

"No," Debbie answered.

"Why are you crying then?"

"I don't know." And then she tried to smile.

The nurse looked over at me. "Don't worry," she said. "This is quite common after surgery."

They got her in the room and I went into high gear, never moving from her bedside. There were ice chips, talking, comforting and slowly through the afternoon, she came around. The nurses were wonderful. Anything we wanted or needed was there. Flowers and cards began to arrive. A girl from work came with insurance papers and with Debbie's help I filled them out and dropped them off at her office the next day. Were they filled out correctly by a mother who was exhausted and half out of her mind and a patient pumped full of pain killers? Your guess. I knew she was a lot better that evening when she asked for her cell phone and ate. Her grandmother and I were in a stupor. The Grueneichs were taking care of the dogs and it was time to get back to Mart. The day came to an end.

Later, I learned Debbie's weight was presenting a huge problem. Yes, morbid obesity. The bacteria had moved into the lower roll of fat around her side and back, just above the buttocks. Since there is poor blood circulation in body fat, the antibiotics were not reaching this area fast enough to kill them. Unbeknownst to me, while in the operating room the surgeon had drawn a line around this area. Sort of like drawing a line in the sand. If the infection crossed this line she was a goner.

No one had mentioned Super Bug: a collection of bacteria including staph and others, picked up in hospitals, schools, gyms and correctional facilities. Anyplace where groups of people live or work together the chance of infection is very high. Infection in a hospital is very common, and a big reason why hospitals want patients released and sent home as soon as possible after surgery. Who are these guys? They're bacteria, and you can't see them. Usually an antibiotic will knock a staph out, but not these guys. They were here to kill people.

Back in Mart, I e-mailed friends in Houston. Don't know when I'll be home as Debbie has a staph infection that's gone nuts. The thing for me to do now, I thought, was to get organized, my specialty.

I fell back on my old reliable ally: organization. Keep all the balls in the air. Walk, water, feed the dogs in the morning, clean up their shit, feed mom and get her to take her pills, see to her hair, bathing, laundry, groceries, back to hospital, back to Mart, feed everyone, try to sleep. Just do it. Don't think, just do it, do it, do it.

The next morning at the hospital I ran into Debbie's primary physician, Dr. Aldridge, in the hallway.

"I think this should have been nailed sooner," he said.

"You think? Look, I didn't bring enough Aricept for my mom's Alzheimer's. Could you write me a prescription since I don't know how long I'm going to be here?"

"Sure, I can do that," he replied. And he did. Right there in the hallway. I got it filled at noon while floundering around Waco looking for a drug store. I knew how to get to the mall and to Mart, and that was it. I think it was that afternoon I began to retreat to the safe place in my mind, the place where I write. Did I pray? I guess so. I don't remember. I was beginning to get numb.

Three: The Fight — Round One

There were no beds available in ICU at that time, so they treated Debbie from the room, as an ICU patient. That's why there was so much nurse/doctor traffic. The next day we still couldn't get into ICU, but a room opened up right next to it, so they moved her there. Visitors told me that if you called the hospital to inquire as to Debbie's progress, you were told she was in ICU. This information was freaking them out but it went right over my head. ICU was for intensive nursing, not for Debbie. I was entering lock-down.

Wednesday and Thursday melted away. I helped Deb bathe and wash her hair. Her incision was just kind of wrapped as they cleaned her out twice a day. As doctors and nurses came and went, Debbie was eating and talking to everyone. She was always so sweet to her nurses, visiting with them and always thanking them for what they did for her. As usual, her spirits were high even though the nurses explained how contagious she was. Everything I did that involved touching her, they insisted I wear gloves. I would rub and touch her feet instead of hugging or kissing her, my own child.

Her grandmother, bless her heart, was holding up well. The three of us talked together a lot, mostly of Debbie going home. At Debbie's home in Mart things were settling into some kind of a pattern. Walk, water, feed the dogs, get mom to take her pills and breakfast. Then I'd shove a load of laundry in the washer, wipe up a little, and off we'd go to the hospital. We'd arrive about eight or nine and spend the rest of the morning with Debbie. After her lunch, I'd take mom out to eat, return for a short visit, then drive back to Mart for a rest and dog walk. By Saturday the pattern was well in place. Now, this is what I could handle. A pattern, a schedule, something I could make sense of. If it doesn't get any worse, I can do this, I thought. It got worse.

Saturday morning, Dr. Yeager was waiting for us.

"The infection is spreading again. There might have to be more surgery and at this point, it's beyond me. I'm going to send her to Grossman Memorial, in Temple. I've already talked to the plastic surgeons there and they're waiting for her. If the fat around her middle, which was where the infection has found a home, has to be removed, plastic surgeons will be needed. The ambulance is here and we'll be preparing her for the trip."

Now, Temple, Texas is another twenty-five miles west of Waco, which would make the round trip from Mart one hundred miles a day. It never crossed my mind that our Debbie would not make a full recovery. I packed up the room and threw her flowers and personal items in the car. I don't remember what Debbie and I said to each other. I only know we talked and were frightened. I had shit for brains by then. Mother knew to some degree what was happening, but she kept very still. Whatever I said, she did. We followed the ambulance to Temple, breaking all speed records.

Four: The Fight — Round Two

The surgery that Dr. Yeager was referring to was similar to the surgery to remove the loose skin on a patient who has had gastric bypass or other surgery for obesity. After a patient loses a lot of weight the skin hangs all over the body and is generally removed by a plastic surgeon. Only this was not loose skin. Under her incision more abscesses were taking hold. The skin was hard and red from the infection, and her temperature was back up to a hundred and one degrees. Jesus Christ, what was happening to my kid?

**

Grossman Memorial Hospital is an old, hulk of a teaching hospital that boasts some of the best medical teams in the state. It is a hospital of specializations and has wings designed for cardiac, cancer, respiratory, plastic surgery, and God knows what else. It's a friendly hospital, lots of people to help you get around this maze of buildings and they will even walk you where you need to go if you look as dazed as I did. The lobby has a cafeteria, donut shop, quick snack shop, and a fresh, hot popcorn stand. The parking lot is so massive they provide free valet parking and shuttles. I was told the hospital was always under construction. A new building was going up just outside the lobby windows and the new cardiac wing had just opened. Temple, Texas, itself, is under construction. At least the freeway system, Highway 35, was and thank God for the blue "H" signs directing me to the hospital, or I would have ended up in Austin. I needed all the help I could get because my heart had found a new home, in my throat.

Debbie was already in her room when we arrived and the new surgical team was there. They ordered all their own tests, asked her and me question after question, examined her again, and consulted. Dr. Ashland, the head of plastic surgery, came back with this plan.

"I know that the doctors at Hartwell expected additional surgery but sometimes that's not the best way to go," he said. "In Debbie's case, we've decided on a wait-and-see procedure for the moment. After her test results come in, we will probably change her antibiotics and watch the new line we've drawn on her."

"Is this life threatening?" I asked.

"Yes, but not as much as it was two days ago."

We waited but had to drive back to Mart. I had dogs to see to and a tired Mother. I walked the floors most of the night. At seven the next morning, we were back at the hospital, waiting. They gave Debbie a pill to ward off a yeast infection from the antibiotics. She'd had a sponge bath but was crazy to get her hair washed.

"Don't worry," said a nurse. "There's a sort of beauty shop down the hall and as soon as she's up I'll take her down there and get her hair washed." And the next day she did just that.

Then Debbie had her period. What a mess. No hospital sanitary belts would fit her so I rinsed out her panties twice a day and dried them over the tub. I also had to do something for Debbie that was hard for me but I slipped on the gloves and got it done: she had trouble cleaning herself after a bowel movement. But, her color was back and she was eating, remarking that the hospital food was great. Later in the day she was up and in a chair, wanting me to bring her nail care bag from home.

Dr. Ashland told me the infection was contained and going down. No more surgery. That night I received an e-mail from Houston. My play, *Sex Games*, had won first prize in the 10x10 Competition. My one thousand dollar prize money was being held for me.

"Way to go, Mom." This was exciting for Debbie.

The next day she was moving about the room, giving orders, mostly to me. I told her I was going to make a break for Houston. I needed to get more medication for Grandma, check the mail, stop the paper, gather up a few more clothes, the dog's heartworm and flea medications and their papers just in case I had to board them. No papers. No boarding. But they had been troopers. No messes in the house. My plan was to spend the morning with Debbie, drive to Houston, stay over and drive back to Mart the next morning, drop off the dogs, and then travel on to Temple. "I'll be here by lunch time," I told her.

"Go," she said. "It's perfect timing. I'm fine here. I'll see you tomorrow."

My ass was dragging but The Morgan Traveling Troupe made the trip and back in record time.

Dr. Ashland and his crew were very pleased with Debbie's progress. They were literally vacuuming her out twice a day. They had her wrapped in a light bandage and someone had come up with a net-like contraption that could stretch around her to keep her secure. The nurse said, "If one thing doesn't work, we find something that will."

Then they introduced us to the wound vac. They were going to try one in the hospital and if all went well they would order her one to take home. This was a machine she'd carry around with her which would be constantly at work cleaning the wound and healing it from the inside out instead of outside in. They fill the wound cavity with sponges, then tape it closed. Then they cut a hole in the tape over the wound, insert a hose, seal the whole thing up and hit "suck" on this machine that you carry on a strap over your shoulder as you go on about your business. Now, this machine will make a beeping sound if the suction sequence is broken and then you have to find the leak and tape over it to seal again until there is no more beeping. Home nursing care would come three times a week to change her cartridge, which was full of very nasty stuff, and monitor her healing, informing the doctor of her progress. We would have extra cartridges in case the vac indicated the cartridge was full and needed to be changed before home nursing got there. And, of course, they'd have to go to Debbie's house from Waco, twenty-five miles away.

On the way home, Mom and I stopped in Waco for lunch. When we got back in the car she seemed uncomfortable. We were just about to swing onto the by-pass to Mart when she said, "I've got to go to the bathroom."

"Why didn't you go in the restaurant?" I asked.

"I didn't have to go then," she answered, as if I was the stupidest person on earth.

"Can you wait until we get to Mart?"

"Nope."

"Okay, there's a hotel over across the expressway. We'll pull in there and use the restroom." I pulled up in their parking lot, went inside and asked to use the bathroom for my mother. No way. There were no service stations that I could see, but Hartwell General Hospital was just down the road and I knew they had a lobby restroom. We pulled in the parking lot, parked the car as close as possible to the entrance and made a dash for it, too late. She had an explosive bowel movement in her pants going down the hospital corridor. I got her inside the restroom and out of her pants, but her underpants were in such a mess there wasn't much I could do but throw them in the trash. I cleaned up her slacks as best I could, got her dressed, and back into the car.

"I've got to go again."

Good Gravy. Back inside we went. Second verse but now the slacks were goners and, for a bonus, her clothes, plus the car, smelled so bad I knew we were going to have to drive with the windows open. The current problem was now my sweet, little English mother was bottomless and stashed inside the hospital restroom. I went out to the car and got the sweater I keep in there in case she got cold in restaurants or movies and brought it inside to wrap around her waist. Checking the hallways and parking lot, I slipped her out of the hospital and back into the car, dropped her hurriedly rinsed slacks on the floor, and drove hell bent for Mart. Can you believe we laughed all the way there?

All went well and by Thursday, August 23rd, Debbie had her own vac and it was working perfectly. Dr. Ashland said she could go home the next day. I started taking her plants and flowers home that day, but not before I told her of her grandmother's sanitary problem of the previous day. We just howled.

Friday, she was released and we drove back to Mart. But with getting in and out of the car and the fifty mile trip, the tape had loosened and just as we pulled into the drive the vac started to beep. I, of course, panicked, but Debbie, cool and calm, had learned her vac lessons well and we soon had her sealed up again. Debbie was tired but like her old self. I made us a nice dinner, walked the dogs, saw to Mom, and collapsed.

***

Saturday, August 25th, Home Care started. Alicia came from Waco and found Debbie's little house easy enough as she had two other patients in the area and she knew Mart well. I went over to Clyde's Grocery to load up on protein foods since Dr. Ashland said she needed protein to heal. While there, I filled in everyone at the store on Debbie's progress. They had all been kept well informed and I'm sure the feeders went out from there. But, no doubt about it, they were wonderful. Nothing was too hard for them to do for me or Debbie. Everything from getting the groceries to the car to saving the choice bits for her. The next day Debbie showered and washed her hair with little help. I popped a roast beef dinner in the oven and we watched movies all afternoon.

Aside from Dukie having a couple of days of the squirts, reminiscent of his human Grandmother, things went along smoothly. Home Care was great and we could depend on them always to be cheerful and competent. They were a Godsend but the ladies needed my help switching out the vac. Climbing up on the bed, it was my job to hold the incision open while the nurse inserted the sponges. Then I helped smooth out the tape to insure Debbie had no leaks.

One night the damned thing went off. For the life of us we couldn't find the leak, but since Home Care was coming the next day, we threw it under a couple of pillows so we couldn't hear it and finally got some sleep.

It was a ghastly wound. I had to swallow hard and will myself not to cry when I did what the nurse asked of me. I had to get over being afraid of it and get over it fast. We had three different nurses: Alicia, Michelle, and Craig. Craig was something else. His hands were so large that he could change Debbie out by himself. He not only trained the other two nurses but me, as well. They taught me the new rules for doing laundry, to always wear gloves, not use the same towel as Debbie, and the cleaning and disposal of her drainage units. And most important of all, was not to forget that we were dealing with an infectious disease. Craig also taught Debbie how to order supplies for the vac and they were delivered to the house by UPS. It was all a hassle, but she was healing and that was the important thing.

During the week Debbie called a coworker, who was a hairdresser, and invited her for dinner. After dinner, we all got haircuts, Mother's hair was a problem, and she looked like she was wearing a fright wig most of the time, so we had it cut short and all I had to do was wash it, blow dry, and go. Debbie's was also cut short so it was easier for her to handle. She was now getting up and dressed.

I'd gotten one of the dates wrong on the Workman's Comp. papers that we'd filled out at the hospital and so we re-did them. Debbie drove herself over to work and dropped them off and visited with a few people for a short time. She was also paying her bills and playing games on the computer.

Sunday, August 9th, I made the drive to Houston, suspecting Debbie was glad to get rid of us for a few days. I had a lot to do back in Houston: clean the house and porch as they were sticky by that time. I had time to visit with my neighbor, who took in my mail and watched over the house. It had rained a couple times a week so the plants and grass were in good shape. I paid bills, talked to some friends, and called Debbie twice a day.

"I'm good," she said. "Stay a few more days."

"I'll be back Wednesday morning." She had a checkup appointment with Dr. Ashland in Temple on the following Wednesday morning.

We made the drive to Temple that morning in good spirits. The doctor looked her over and reported she was doing well. There was no temperature, no swelling, and she was healing nicely. He was very pleased. Also he had been taking pictures of Debbie throughout this ordeal to present to the Plastic Surgeons Association Conference slated for later in the year. Debbie had given him permission and felt quite the celebrity.

Over the next week, we ran into a problem: a tape problem. The tape they were using to secure the incision was causing sores on Debbie's skin. When they removed the tape it took some of her skin with it and those spots had festered. Now there were ulcers around the wound. They ordered a new tape. This one was supposed to not irritate the skin. Why didn't they use it before? It was better but not good.

That week we had a spa day and I did pedicures for her and Mom; stuck their feet in a bucket and clipped away.

*****

September 18th was Debbie's birthday. I made a nice dinner and we all agreed that this year was the pits and next year we were going to throw a blast for everyone. Her cell phone was hot. She talked to friends all around Texas, coworkers, college friends, her dad in Rochester, New York, her half brother and sister, and their kids. She already had Christmas gifts for them in the closet ready to mail, books and games she had found. Aunt Debbie always put a lot of thought every year into their Christmas presents as she enjoyed doing it and lovingly mailed everything off in November of each year.

The next day Home Care came and, while I was helping Alicia with the vac, I felt a hard lump at one end of the incision. It also looked red.

"What's this?" I asked.

"Oh, that's just scar tissue and nothing to worry about." I let it go as Debbie's temperature was normal and she was going to see Dr. Ashland in two days. I made a mental note to ask him to check it out.

At this point, I felt like I wanted to just run away from all this illness. Mother's Alzheimer, my fear, and Dukie's squirts. I slept on the sofa all the time, so Dukie was getting me up all night to go outside. Poor little guy. I wanted to run someplace, any place, but where? Maybe home and pull the covers up over my head? But I knew I couldn't do that. I had to stick it out.

The next day I was putting laundry away in Debbie's room and she was fooling with her angel cards, which she did almost every day. Her angel cards were an over-sized deck of cards lavishly detailed with beautiful angles and each one had an inspirational message from the angel featured on the card. Debbie would shuffle the deck, draw three cards, one each for past, present, and future, and happily read how to solve the problem she had brought to them that day. She was on the bed dealing away as I was sorting the clothes when she suddenly looked up at me and said, "Don't worry, mom, my angels are all around me."

They were, too, only I didn't know it then.

Five: Taking It Up A Notch

Apparently, Dr. Ashland and Home Care had been discussing the use of the tape that was causing ulcers around Debbie's incision. It was pealing her skin off when it was replaced and that was happening three times a week. Her skin continued to fester, even with the new tape. So due to the fact that the incision had closed substantially and she was doing so well, Dr. Ashland decided to go ahead and close her up the following Friday.

We were all so excited, especially Debbie, as she was so tired of lugging around her beep freak vac friend. Just going to the bathroom was a hassle, not to mention showering. Getting rid of it, besides closing her up, was a big step toward her total recovery. Since she was going to have to be very careful of her stitches and staples and would have to stay quiet while healing, we went shopping and bought a TV for her bedroom. She had a cable outlet and her neighbor, Hershel, hooked it up for us.

Friday, September 21st, we drove to Temple. It was an overcast day. A skinny sun was hardly breaking through moody clouds as we swung around our familiar route. The air was cool and I could almost smell rain in the air. I was glad September was winding down.

Dr. Ashland was doing this final procedure as an outpatient and Debbie would be able to come home the same day. He had thought he might have to graft some skin off her thigh to properly close her but it wasn't necessary. He inserted two internal drains that attached to two small plastic bottles outside the incision. These were at each end of the closing stitches and they just popped on and off. These bottles had measurements on them and they had to be removed twice a day and the drainage in the bottles measured and recorded. Then the bottles were cleaned and snapped back on the tubes. We were to take the recorded measurements with us on our next office visit.

As Debbie was coming out of the anesthetic he took me aside and told me he had had to remove another abscess from the cavity and he was still concerned about reinfection. I told him about the hard lump I had felt a few days before and that the home nurse had told me it was scar tissue. He just shook his head. "We'll watch it very closely," he said. My stomach turned over but I wouldn't give in to it. I would not accept in any way that Debbie was not going to fully recover. This was just a blip and I quickly involved myself with her getting over the anesthetic and getting her home.

Now, this closing surgery was not done at Grossman Memorial but at a small out-patient clinic a few blocks away from the hospital. Since it was a small clinic they didn't have a wheelchair big enough for Debbie so we put her in an office chair on casters and rolled her out the door. She had to walk about five or so steps to the car. She did it with our help and we got her settled in the back seat and headed for Mart. The weather had cleared and the sun was shining. Debbie was very quiet on the ride home and when we quickly got her into her own bed she instantly fell asleep.

***

Friday, Saturday, and Sunday we did the drain thing, ate light meals, and stayed quiet. Debbie watched her TV, read, and kept busy with her angel cards. We talked about a lot of things like her coming home, putting her things in storage until she was on her feet, and then renting an apartment in Houston. I felt it was way past time for her not to be so far away from home.

Monday morning we had an appointment with Dr. Ashland to check her over and give him the report on her drainage. At two a.m. Monday morning. Debbie came out to me where I was sleeping on the sofa.

"Don't freak out, Mom, but you need to call an ambulance. Something's wrong. I can't breathe right." Her hands were trembling.

"Look, I can get you to the emergency room at Hartwell General faster than we can wait for an ambulance to get to Mart and then drive you to Waco. Get in the car just as you are and let's go."

I ran the dogs out for a quick pee, told Mom I was taking Debbie to the hospital and that we'd be home soon and off we went. Leaving Mom alone was very dangerous at this point but I had no choice. I didn't know what was waiting for me.

I ran inside the emergency ward quickly finding someone to help me.

"I need a big wheelchair," I cried out. One was promptly provided and we got Debbie inside and into an examining room. Her breathing was labored and they put her on oxygen, a drip, and began running tests. It took three times for a nurse to try and find a vein. No good. They had to go through the neck again. They did blood, EKG, MRI and whatever as I walked the floors. All tests came back negative. For the first time during this whole thing that I remembered, I prayed. There, alone, in the examining room, while they were running the tests I was on my knees. God, what's going on here? Please keep me calm. Help me to stay focused and do what needs to be done. Please, God, help me. This is beyond me. Lots of thoughts, but mostly about me, me, me.

Two hours later the diagnosis: acid reflux, and see Dr. Aldridge ASAP. We got a prescription filled at the all-night pharmacy and drove back to Mart, needing to rest. We had breakfast when we got home and then left again for an eight forty-five appointment with Dr. Ashland, in

Temple. When he entered the examining room he saw a Debbie he had not seen before. We told him of our trip to the emergency room and the diagnosis.

"Get in to see Dr. Aldridge today," he said. "This is not my field at all."

He examined Debbie. I knew by the way he looked her over he was considering admitting her. Compared to her last visit she looked like hell. She had no color, appeared washed out, and was slumped over in the chair. No smile, no greeting, no jokes, no nothing, just a very sick girl. After visually making up his mind, he said he was going to change her medication and wanted her back in two days.

On the way home we got all the prescriptions filled, picked up some sandwiches for lunch, and headed for Mart. We were all exhausted and I fell asleep on the sofa. While I rested, Debbie called Dr. Aldridge's office and she woke me up saying we had a four- thirty afternoon appointment. So we all piled back in the car again.

Dr. Aldridge called, checked with the emergency room doctor, and got her test results. He informed us everything was done for her as he would have ordered. He concurred with their acid reflux diagnosis and then threw in an anxiety attack for good measure. "No wonder," he said, "Debbie has been pushing all this down someplace and is now just reacting to it. This is quite a normal reaction to her situation." He gave her a prescription for anxiety to help calm her down when she needed it. We headed to the pharmacy for the third time that day, then for take-out BBQ and home. I was all focus and single mindedness. The depth of my concentration could have moved trees.

"You get a gold star for mother today," Debbie said, and went to bed.

***

Debbie started her new meds on September 26th and by the next day she was a different person.

"Mom," she said, "after I took this new pill I felt a warm sensation going all through my body."

I told her how hard I had prayed for her in the emergency room and maybe this was an answer to my prayers. It never occurred to me that it could be the new meds or that maybe she and my mom had also been praying. It was still all about me.

Two days later, back to Temple and Dr. Ashland.

"Look, I brought you a new girl from two days ago," I said to the doctor.

She was alert, laughing and joking with him. He examined her and said we would continue as we were. There were no new lumps, no swellings, and her skin was a normal color. Drains were doing well and secretion levels were going down.

The final few days of September were wonderful. Debbie even drove to Waco by herself to get her hair colored and a pedicure. The next day she drove to the post office, went to the store, paid her bills, sat at her computer, and talked about going over to her office for a scheduled short meeting the next day. I was thanking God and e-mailing Houston: coming home soon.

It was October. The weather cool, the leaves on Debbie's big tree beginning to turn crimson and yellow. The footballs were flying and, according to Sam, Debbie's landlord, the Mart football team was unbeatable this season. Debbie spent a lot of time out on the patio reading, on her computer playing games or on the phone to everyone. I felt she was getting tired of Mom and me being around all the time. Perfectly understandable for a person well on the road to recovery and wanting her privacy back. Life would soon be back to normal.

Six: October, The Month That Was

Monday, October 1st, Debbie got up early. We had breakfast together and while I walked our furry pains-in-the-butt she got dressed and drove over to her office to see everyone. She had just learned she had a new boss and she wanted to meet her in person and do a little paperwork. She looked good, healthy and upbeat, and was more than ready to return to work and normalcy. Tuesday and Wednesday there was just more improvement. There was little drainage now and she was doing a little cleaning up of the house and some cooking.

"Are you ready for a few days alone?" I asked.

"I sure am. I love you dearly, but I've lived alone for so long I need some time to myself." I made a few meals for her freezer.

Thursday, October 4th, we all drove to Temple for a checkup appointment with Dr. Ashland. He removed all her drains. "Doctor, I asked, "Was this that Super Bug, that MRSA, that's been in all the news lately?"

"Sure was, but Debbie is completely recovered and can return to work November 1st. I just want her to take the rest of the month off to completely heal. If you need me I'm here, but as far as I'm concerned she's released." He took his final pictures and we all said goodbye to him, Temple, and Grossman Memorial Hospital. It was glorious.

It rained like hell coming home. It was one of those Texas downpours where you can't see past the hood of the car and you have to pull over to the side of the road. Turning on my flashers so I wouldn't get hit in the rear, we waited it out. The sun soon pushed its way through sluggish gray clouds and we stopped for lunch in Waco and did a little shopping.

While driving to the mall I felt something rolling around my mouth. Pulling it out I realized half of one of my teeth had fallen out. It didn't hurt but, shit, what next? Friday, the next day, I left for Houston and my dentist.

***

The rain in Houston had gone south so most of my plants were dried up skeletons and the grass was a brown patch disaster. Quickly getting Mom and I settled at home, I called the dentist for an emergency appointment and did some grocery shopping. I needed everything. Every dash to Mart meant I stripped my fridge and took it with me. Debbie had decided to spend the weekend at Lake Conroe to visit her cousins as she needed different conversation and company than her old mom and grandmother. She planned to drive into Houston to spend a few days at home the following Monday morning.

She arrived while I was at my dental appointment. I was totally looking at a root canal and crown at this point, but my dentist, bless his heart, saved it. Thank God I wasn't tied up for a couple weeks with a tooth because the next morning Debbie got up and said, "Mom, come look. What in hell's this all over me?"

"Looks like hives to me." I answered, looking her over. She had red blotches and they itched like hell. I went over to the drug store which was four blocks away remembering the twenty-five mile Waco trip, and bought some Benadryl and a tube of cream for the itching. Nothing helped. It got worse. Her feet, hands, face, neck— her whole body was a swollen red welt and by the end of the day she was half out of her mind with the scratching. I put her in a cool bath, slathered her with creams and pumped in the Benadryl. Early Tuesday morning, three a.m. to be exact, we were on our way to the emergency room at Hoover Medical Center. I took all the medications she was taking with us. The diagnosis: acute hives. What had caused this? A combination of all the medications she'd been taking for two months? The doctor went over everything, substituting some meds and stopping others. Wednesday and Thursday she wasn't much better and she had big sores on her body from scratching. It was back to the emergency room and the same doctor. This time he gave her a shot and a high-powered antihistamine. She got better, but Friday afternoon I called Dr. Aldridge and told him what was going on.

"Keep doing what you're doing and be in my office at nine-thirty Monday morning. I may have to send her to an allergist"

Saturday and Sunday the swelling went down and the itching was under control. The anxiety pills helped to keep her calm. The worst was over it seemed. Sunday afternoon she drove back to Mart and I followed the next morning. When I got there at eight-thirty a.m. she was sitting in her living room, a total mess.

"I've been up half the night trying to meditate and keep myself together. I just kept saying, 'Mom will be here soon.'" This was something different. It looked like an anxiety attack to me, but what the hell did I know? She was in tears and highly agitated. I called Dr. Aldridge, and he took her in immediately. The hives were under control and the sores were healing without her scratching them open constantly. But, to be on the safe side, he made the appointment with the allergist. This was October 15th.

Later that night, another three a.m. call. Casey came over to the sofa where I slept and I figured he just wanted to go out. I reached out to pet him with a, "Hold on, big boy, I'm coming." In the dark I touched his head; it was as big as a cow's! I got up and turned on the light and what a sight. Something must have bitten him on one of his trips down the alley where I walked both dogs. There were a lot of bushes and a pile of wood and junk behind the Grueneich's garage where he poked around all the time. Maybe it had been a scorpion, a spider, or even a snake. Whatever it had been, he had a full blown reaction to something and neither dog's food had been changed. At six I started calling vets. At seven I contacted one and explained what I thought had happened to him.

"Bring him right in. We'll be waiting." I even knew where the vet's clinic was located. It was a block from Hartwell General Hospital.

Mom woke Debbie and she insisted on coming with me. She was a little slow moving but very concerned about Casey. He slept with her while we were in Mart and climbed in with her when she was in Houston as well. The vet was great and confirmed it was some sort of bite and he'd be fine. Then I got the bill: one hundred dollars.

The next day, Wednesday the 17th, Debbie was up and about and cutting down on the anxiety pills. She was enjoying her meals, showering, washing her hair and even shaved her legs. Her incision was healing beautifully. Her skin looked normal and there was no swelling. Casey's swollen head was going down. I was going to make spaghetti for dinner and things were hunky-dory.

Next morning I awakened Debbie.

"Come and look at this dog. The swelling's gone down, but look, it's settled in under his chin." There was a large, hard, lump under Casey's chin the size of a baseball. "What do you think?" We went back to the vet. She lanced it, gave me pain pills and antibiotics and another bill, this time for two hundred dollars. Debbie and I just looked at each other but I thought we got off cheap. I sent them a thank-you card.

For the rest of the week things went pretty smoothly. Debbie popped right back to her old self. Sunday, the 21st, we drove to Waco for lunch and a movie. Then we stopped off at Wal-Mart for paper goods and I picked up a birthday present for her grandmother. I noticed Debbie's breathing was elevated and she had to sit down while I got the supplies. When I asked her about it she said she was just tired and I didn't think too much about it. After all she had been through the past weeks, I figured she had a perfect right to be tired and, as always, she was in good humor. That night Grandma went to bed early, the dogs settled down, and while munching on pop corn we watched a comedy show. We were both half crying from laughing at Jim Dunham and his very naughty puppets. Life was good again.

The next day I was exhausted and Debbie knew it. She was up and dressed and had plans to clean up a few things at the house. Casey was healing and was off his pain pills and antibiotics.

"Mom, are you ready to go home?"

"I guess so. The dog thing did me in."

"I know, and Grams wants to sleep in her own bed."

"I do, too" I answered. I'd been on her sofa for almost three months.

"Why don't you drive on home today? I've got that nine a.m. appointment with the allergist tomorrow and then I'll just come on into Houston."

"I don't want you to drive to Temple and the allergist by yourself. I thought you were going to follow me into Houston after we got back or Wednesday morning."

"I'll be fine. Besides I want to spend a little time at Lake Conroe visiting with Pam,"—her cousin—"and then I'll come on home for a few days."

"You're sure?"

"Yeah, then I've planned to drive back here on Sunday. I need a few days alone to get myself ready to go back to work on Thursday."

So Debbie and I packed up all my and Grandma's gear, including all our meds, the dog's meds, food and toys, plus all the things I had accumulated over the past three months. All the crap I had duplicated so I hadn't had to bring so much back and forth. We loaded my car to the hilt and Debbie started cleaning her house around me. Mom and I got in the car and we mentally said "so long" to Mart, Texas, and headed for Houston. When we got home I unloaded everything, put it away, and went to have the car washed. There were four layers of Mart mud smothering it.

Tuesday I started cleaning the house. The porch was a mess again and I had a ton of laundry. Later in the day, Debbie pulled into the driveway. She'd been to the allergist who contributed "zero" to the problem, then enjoyed a short visit in Conroe, Texas.

"Want to go to the movies and grab some dinner out?" I asked her.

"Naaa. Not today. I just want to lie around and enjoy the day at home."

And that we did. We fired up the DVD and watched movies, had hamburgers on the porch, opened a bottle of non-alcoholic sparkling cider to celebrate her recovery, and we all went to bed just as a blazing sun set.

The next day we were all up early for a light breakfast.

"How about running over to the Central Market today and bringing home dinner?" I asked. "We could eat out on the porch again." Central Market is located in the "got rocks" section of Houston. It's a gourmet market and very pricy, but it has everything, from everywhere, and a huge specialty pre-cooked department. There is everything from chicken cordon-bleu to stuffed quail eggs. That was right up our alley.

"That sounds great."

So off we went, Grams, Debbie, and I, to the market and picked up salads, exotic olives, hard rolls and a fruit tart. I took her car and got it washed and we just piddled around the rest of the day. That evening we hauled our goodies out to the porch for dinner. It was a beautiful October evening. The air had a hint of jasmine and we just settled back.

Debbie didn't eat much as we celebrated Mom's birthday a few days early. Mom's ninety-first birthday was the following Monday and Debbie would not be with us then. She'd be back in Mart getting ready to go back to work and my lifeboat would be moored in a safe harbor.

It had been announced on the news that day that the space shuttle could be seen that night coming over Houston, so I watched for it. It was almost dark when I spotted it and called Debbie and Mom outside. It was one of those Texas pink and blue twilights. It seemed an effort for Debbie to come out into the yard and she seemed disinterested. Her breathing was labored, and I commented on it.

"How come you're breathing so hard?"

"It's just my Houston allergies acting up."

We went to bed early, but my radar was up and working. She didn't look good.

Seven: Losing Sight Of Normal

Thursday morning my guts were in turmoil. I'd had a restless night and knew things were not right. What was going on I asked myself as I had coffee on a dark porch. What have I missed? What should I be doing that I'm not doing? I walked the dogs and made cheese and sausage rolls for breakfast. Mom got up and we had a roll while reading the paper, neither of us saying much. Debbie came into the kitchen about an hour later.

"Want some breakfast, sweetheart?"

"No, not yet, Mom. I don't feel very good this morning."

I knew she had slept most of the night in the big chair in front of the TV. She could breathe more comfortably and would sleep there a lot when she was home and then go off to her own bed when I got up with the, we're hungry and got to pee dog parade.

"Why don't you try taking one of your anxiety pills and a reflux and go on back to bed for a while and we'll see what happens?" Nothing happened. She spent the morning in the recliner. That afternoon I called Dr. Aldridge.

"Double up on the reflux pills," he suggested. Okay, we did that and waited. Everyone and everything on hold and me watching her like a hawk. I was weighing and wondering and thinking about packing up again and hauling everyone's ass back to Mart.

Oh, my God. Not back to Mart, to sleeping on the sofa, to the marathon trips to the drug store and doctors. Not so soon, please, I can't take all that again.

Later that afternoon, as I watched her napping in the recliner, I noticed her breath was coming fast and hard and she had a gray look about her. I really saw her for the first time in a long time. She was enormous, completely filling the large recliner, struggling to breath and snoring like a longshoreman. Suddenly a voice as clear as someone standing next to me whispered in my head, "You're going to lose her." I backed up a few steps and said right out loud, "No way is that going to happen. I won't allow that to happen."

The next day, Friday, she seemed better but I noticed her sitting on my bed after a trip to the bathroom off my bedroom. It will all be okay, I told myself again. This will all pass like all the other setbacks.

"What's the matter, honey?"

"It's nothing, just my morning allergies draining." But I'd noticed she started coughing, and sometimes deeply. Like croup. We took it real slow and easy that day, but she had no appetite and was real jumpy and was short with me at times, which was so unlike her. It was almost like she resented me hovering.

Later, I said to her, "What's that lump on your forehead?"

"I bumped it in the bathroom this morning."

"You fell on the floor?"

"No, I was on the toilet and just toppled over a little and bumped my head on the towel rack.

"Do you think we should go back to Mart and go see Dr. Aldridge Monday?"

"Nah, it's okay. I'm fine. Let's just stick to the meds and see how it goes."

I noticed her hands were trembling a little. Was she weak? This has just all caught up to her. She needs time to physically and emotionally get over this. Lots of rest. Here at home.

"I think you'd better consider taking more time off. What do you think?"

"I don't think I have much more time to take off."

"That's tough shit. Take it without pay. I'll take care of what we need to pay."

"Well, it's a thought."

"Debbie, there's no way you can go back to work Thursday."

"You might be right. I really don't feel that good."

She had no temperature and no hives. She was just very tired and breathing deep. She slept in the chair again. It was a long night.

Saturday was a nightmare of worry. She didn't seem worse but not better, either. The anxiety pills and acid reflux didn't seem to be working.

"You're going to Waco to the hospital today."

"Please, Mom, one more day. Give the pills a chance to work."

"Okay, but if you're not better in the morning, we're on our way."

I was beside myself wondering what to do. I knew she didn't want to go back into the hospital. The thought of yet another doctor's appointment was incomprehensible to her. I tried to console her. "Don't worry about one thing. We'll all just stay in Mart until you're feeling better and then we'll just put everything in storage and come on back to Houston. There are a lot of jobs in Houston. When you're better you'll get one and we'll find you a cute little apartment and bring your stuff here. The thing now is to get you feeling better. We'll get you a doctor here in Houston even if we have to go to Medicaid. You don't have to worry about money."

I was babbling. I was frantic. If this was allergies and she needed extensive testing, I had to get her back to Mart where her insurance would kick in. If it was something else, I still had to get her back to her own doctors where all her medical records were. Where there were doctors that knew her history and could go over everything. I was guessing. What in hell did I know? I was half out of my mind.

I started gathering up things to take, Mom's things, the dogs' things, my things, Debbie's things. It all had to go into my car somehow because she couldn't drive, but I'd be prepared this time and I knew how to pack. Debbie could not seem to eat although I tempted her with foods she liked. She said she felt a lot of congestion and I ran to the drug store for Mucinex.

We all slept poorly. I walked my bedroom and Mom wandered the house. In the morning I made Debs some oatmeal with brown sugar and milk. She came to the table but just pushed the food around. She sat in the recliner to watch the Sunday morning news while I was mentally packing the car.

Suddenly, "Mom, I'm going to throw up." I grabbed my wicker bathroom waste basket just in time, but it was only phlegm. I took her temp. Normal. She started to gag again but only brought up more phlegm. I wiped her face with a cool washcloth.

"That's it. We're going back to Mart now and you're going immediately to the emergency ward." I had the car packed in fifteen minutes, threw Mom and the dogs in the back, Debbie and her bucket in the front, and we were on our way. I drove like hell and we were all very quiet except for me saying, "Back to Mart, the bad luck town." Like everyone needed to hear that crap.

We got to Mart in record time. I ran Mom and the dogs inside; a quick pee for me, then the dogs down the alley. I told Debbie to just pee by the side of the car if she had to go. She couldn't have made it into the house.

"Hurry, Mom," she pleaded.

In just a few minutes Debbie and I were on our way to Hartwell General Hospital's emergency ward in Waco. Again, in record time, I pulled into the parking lot and ran inside. It was a miracle I wasn't stopped and ticketed.

"I need a large wheelchair right away. My daughter's in the car and is very sick."

They were there in a minute or so. She was soon admitted and in a room where tests were begun. I was so frightened I could hardly talk. My stomach was so cramped I was slumped over, and I was half crazy with fear. What's going on now? What is it this time?

In came the doctors, nurses, and IV's. Debbie talked to them, telling them how she felt. She signed the papers they brought to her. Then she felt nauseous again. They gave her a shot to control it and she slowly began to settle down.

"They better find out what's wrong with me, Mom, because I can't be sick like this anymore." Then she drifted off to babble incoherently.

A doctor came in. "Our tests are indicating a gall bladder attack."

I leaned over Debbie. "It's okay," I whispered to her. "Maybe just gall bladder. That's what's making you so sick. You're going to be fine. Even if it means taking it out they do all that by laser now, out-patient stuff. We're home free now."

"I'm thirsty, Mom."

"Okay, I'll run get us a Sprite with ice. How's that?"

"Great."

On my way to the cafeteria, I passed one of the doctors and said, "I've never seen her so sick in her whole life."

The doctor just looked at me. "She's pretty sick, all right," he agreed.

When I got back with the Sprite and ice, Dr. Yeager, dressed in street clothes, was in Debbie's cubicle. He looked as if he'd just gotten off the golf course. This was the surgeon who had done the original staph operations on her in August. Who had called him? Obviously, from the way he was dressed, someone at the hospital.

"What do you think?" I asked.

"Don't know yet." He was going over her.

Debbie was answering his questions, but the shot was making it hard for her to focus. Her answers were becoming fuzzy so I answered his questions as best I could.

"Are you going to admit her?"

"Yes, but not here. Whatever this is, it's not gall bladder. I've sent for an ambulance to transport her back to Temple and Grossman where the experts are. I don't like the look of her legs."

Debbie responded to the Temple remark and we just looked at each other. I don't know what she was thinking, but I was putting the one hundred mile round trip to Temple in perspective. Again, the trips to the hospital, the caring for Mom and the dogs; I was getting mentally prepared. In an instant, we both accepted it and knew this is what it was going to be and my mind clicked into "cope" gear. The time change had just taken place: we had lost an hour of daylight and it was beginning to get dark. You can put my night driving skills in a thimble, and Mom and the dogs were back in the house in Mart. What to do? Follow the ambulance to Temple or go back to Mart and take care of what I had to there?

The gurney arrived. "Okay, you're in good hands now. I'm going back to the house to take care of Grandma and the dogs, and ask Sam and Alice to look after them. I'll call you when you get to your room and we'll take it from there."

"You go on, Mom, I'll be okay now." The nausea had stopped and she was talking to me normally. She climbed up on the gurney with a little help from the paramedics and, as they maneuvered her into the hall, she joked with them and was on her way.

"I'll call you in a little while," I called after her.

"Okay. Talk to you later."

I drove back to Mart, told Mom what was going on, then called Grossman Hospital, in Temple, and asked for Debbie. She sounded okay, so I walked the dogs, got into her bed and, surprisingly, dozed off.

Eight: October 29th — Gram's Birthday

At five a.m. I was up walking hairy critters down the dark alley. It was cool now and the morning air smelled like pine cones and old earth. I made Mom and me a little breakfast, fed the beasts, and gassed up. We were at Grossman by seven a.m. The first thing I noticed when entering the hospital was that Debbie had been assigned to the cardiac wing. Why? Calm down, calm down, was all I could think to tell myself. I knew I would know the story when I looked at her and heard her talk to me.

I entered her room and she was sitting up in bed talking to a nurse. I noticed a catheter and, of course, the IV's.

"Hi, Mom, this is Patty. She lives in College Station."

"And you drive fifty miles here every day?" I asked the green-clad Patty.

"Sure do."

I got my mom settled into an over-stuffed chair and looked Debbie over.

"So what's going on in here today?" I questioned.

"They ran tests most of the night, Mom. Its blood clots in my legs. They're dissolving them now. One got to one of my lungs."

I gulped but didn't see anything unusual going on in the room. She spit up a little and I wiped her mouth with a warm washcloth. It was just phlegm. She hadn't eaten, so I got her a Popsicle. A team of doctors came in just then but they didn't ask us to leave. Remember, this is a teaching hospital and these doctors were young, young, young. They kidded around with us, saying Debbie had told them about Central Market and lunch on the porch. Debbie was cheerful and talkative. They informed me about the blood clots and that they were pumping her full of Heparin to dissolve them and a nurse would be in later to explain the procedure.

A little later the nurse arrived and told us that Debbie and I would be trained on how to give a Heparin shot to her as she would need to keep up the treatment when she got home. *When she got home.* These were the words I welcomed and understood. I told her I'd be there with Debbie to give her the shots as long as they were needed. She was given a sponge bath and a clean gown and for a while she napped. She's been up all night with the tests and was tired. She drifted in and out of sleep, watched a little TV, and was going to have a little soup and Jell-O for lunch. A nurse came in and said they were going to remove the catheter that afternoon and have her sitting up in the big lounge chair that Mom was currently lost in. About two p.m., I decided to take Mom back to

41

Mart, get some lunch, and take care of the dogs. Then I'd get the neighbors to look in on them and drive back to the hospital and stay the night. Debbie woke up and was getting ready to have her lunch as I told her the plan. "What do you think?"

"Sounds good, but don't rush around. I'm fine here with all these nurses. Just get me another popsicle before you go."

"I'll be back late this afternoon. I'll call you when I'm on my way." Mom and I got up to leave. We both hugged her and, as I turned at the door, she said, "I'll see you later, Mother."

We left the hospital, stopping for a quick lunch in Waco. When we got to Debbie's house, Mom went to lie down and I did the dog thing. Only this time I had to go down the alley picking up all the mess they'd left the last two days. There was a neighbor on the other side of the alley who was complaining that I didn't clean up after them, which I did every day or so. He was a nasty sort of fellow with a big mouth. Like all I had on my mind right now was dog shit. I tried to explain to him about Debbie's illness and our trips to the hospital but he didn't want to hear that. He only wanted to talk about calling the sheriff if the dogs crapped in his yard again. Apparently, he was the Mart dog shit expert, so I didn't bother to tell him that my dogs' mess was at that moment in the trash can and I could give a rat's ass whose dog was shitting in his yard. What a jerk!

I called Debbie and she said she had eaten a little and the catheter had been removed." I'm going to get Sam and Alice to look after Grams and maybe run the dogs out, then I'm going to take a little rest and drive back in."

"Cool. I talked to Dad and Helen. And I called work. They're doing all the paperwork again."

At five p.m. I called her.

"I have to go to the bathroom, so call me back in a little while." She sounded annoyed. "Damn it, I just peed on the floor. I'll talk to you later."

***

"Wait a sec. Have you been up in the chair?"

"Not yet, but after I pee again, that's the plan. Then I have to call Alex, a co-worker, and make sure everyone knows I'm not coming back Thursday or maybe the following week."

I made arrangements for Mom and the dogs with Casey and put a blanket and pillow in the car for the night shift at the hospital. Then I called Debbie to tell her I was on my way. A nurse answered. It threw me a little but I figured if Debs was in the chair maybe the nurse was closest to the phone.

"This is Debbie's Mom. Is she there?"

"The doctor is here and I'll put him on."

"Mrs. Levy? Debbie's having a lot of trouble breathing and I'm taking her to the ICU to insert a trachea. You'd better come."

My stomach lurched. "I'm in Mart, about an hour away. I'm leaving right now."

I ran the dogs out, made Mom a sandwich, and told her I was going to the hospital but she couldn't come this time because I was spending the night with Debbie. I told her Alice and Sam would look in on her. The car clock read six p.m. when I pulled out of the driveway. Twilight was fast approaching. I drove like a mad woman.

Out on the highway, I tried to pass a car on the left side and. *WHAM,* there was debris on the road right in front of me that almost sent me into the ditch. Sweet Jesus, not a wreck, not now. Pulling hard on the wheel, I righted the car and slowed down a little, enough to match my heartbeat. Go. Go. Go.

# Nine: Angels For A Birthday

The familiar landmarks were quickly going by as I drove well over the speed limit. There was the Church of Christ on the right with the old-fashioned steeple. Then Andy's Car Swap and the spidery power lines that warned me the interstate was approaching.

Just before I arrived at the Waco by-pass, Highway 35 to Temple, my left turn signal suddenly started blinking. Click-click, Click-click, Click-click. God damn it, what in hell's wrong with the car, I thought. It blinked six or seven times then stopped. I tested the signals, first right and then left; they worked fine. It was probably just a short somewhere. This was just what I needed right then car trouble. Then a thought entered my mind. A strong thought—more than a thought—a voice, wiping out everything else.

"Look at the time. The clock on the dash. This is important."

I did and the car clock read six-twenty p.m.

A voice in my mind screamed, *"Something is very wrong here. Hurry, hurry."*

The air in the car seemed very close and I found myself struggling for breath. I opened my window, let in the cool evening air, turned up the car radio, and floored it.

It was now really starting to get dark; I drove like a fiend, fear clutching my guts. Something's wrong. Something's wrong. The western sky was ablaze on the horizon and lights were coming on in Waco as I zoomed around the bypass and into the final stretch. Highway 35 to Temple - twenty-five more miles.

Reaching the hospital parking lot, I checked the time. It was seven p.m. Running between the cars and into the hospital, I went directly to the ICU ward. It wasn't visiting hours and the waiting room was filled with people in chairs, sofas, and some sleeping on the floor, waiting to see loved ones. Good thing I'd brought a blanket and pillow, because it looked like this was where I would be spending the night. Someone told me that if I rang the buzzer on the wall someone would answer and send a nurse to help me. It seemed a foggy world to me. The situation was real, but hazy. I pressed the buzzer and someone indeed answered. I told them who I was and that the doctors had told me to come immediately.

"Just stay right there." I was told. "Someone will be down to take you in."

Through the large windows I could see it was now dark, but the lights from the parking lot cast a yellow glow across the parked cars. I began to pace when suddenly a voice from behind me said, "Mrs. Levy?"

Two doctors were standing there.

"Yes," I answered.

"Please come this way." I followed. And out of the blue it came, "Please God, help me through this."

They escorted me into a conference room and we all stood next to a long, polished, mahogany table. There were no windows in the room and a chair had been pulled out.

I took a deep breath. "How's she doing?"

They began to talk and I began to drift away.

"Debbie had blood clots in her legs."

"Debbie had clots in her lungs and one traveled to the heart"

"Debbie had a cardio-respiratory failure."

"Debbie had a massive pulmonary embolism."

I couldn't breathe. "Debbie *had*," I was yelling. "Are you telling me she's gone?"

They nodded. Then I knew why the chair had been pulled out; because I collapsed into it. Oh, my God, this could not be happening. I don't believe this. The rest came in bits and pieces. I was pulling away mentally and physically as I strained to push away from the doctors.

"We worked on her for forty-five minutes. There was nothing we could do. These things happen so fast. She was gone before we could get the trachea in but she was asleep when she passed. I hope that's a comfort to you."

This was a comfort? I was crying and babbling as I tried to tell them about the blinker going off in the car and how I had known there was something wrong, but no one understood what I was saying.

Another doctor came, then a minister.

"Is there anyone we can call?" They circled me in a ring of white coats.

"Yes, her dad, in New York." I somehow found the number. Boxes of Kleenex arrived. My voice sounded like I was in a tunnel.

A doctor asked, "A funeral home?"

All this was coming in waves. I told them that years ago she had donated her body to science but I couldn't remember who it was. I could only recall the arguments we had regarding it.

"I can't do that, Debbie." I'd told her, really mad.

"Yes, you can, Mom, It's what I want," she declared, just as mad.

Thank God, I thought, from my dark, isolated place, I'm not going to have to deal with this. I'll just go along with Debbie now so she won't be alone.

"We'll check all this out for you," said one of the doctors, as he ran for a computer.

I kind of pulled myself together for a moment and then they brought me her ring and watch in a baggie and I slipped down into the darkness again.

"Where's her cell phone?" I asked, stupidly. Like it mattered.

The minister talked to me, but I didn't hear a word he said. Then they led me out of the room so I could see her. I got as far as the visiting room door of the ICU and balked.

"No." I pulled away from them and saw that the people in the waiting room were watching me, three doctors, and a minister. "No. I can't see her like that. I want to remember her laughing."

"That's fine," one of the doctors said, and we went back into the conference room. They had been on the net and had contacted the Texas State University Medical Branch in Dallas. Would they take Debbie? Yes. There had been no answer at her dad's.

I stood up. "I have to go home now. I have to go tell my mother that her beloved only grandchild has died on her birthday."

Somehow I got out of there and the minister walked with me to the parking lot. The air was heavy around me and I felt crowded, but there was only the two of us standing next to the car.

"Are you going to be all right?"

"Yes." My eyes dried as I put a box of Kleenex on the seat. "I have to get to my Mother."

"Now, just pull over if you start to cry again. Promise me that."

"I promise. I'll be fine."

I got into the car and it felt warm and again crowded. It was hard to breathe, and as I pulled out of the hospital parking lot, I again rolled down the window and turned up the radio—real loud—and in a dry-eyed trance began the trip back to Mart.

I drove slow and sure. When I pulled onto Highway 35 I got behind a big truck and followed him to Waco. I must stay focused and drive slow, were my thoughts. My only goal that night was to now get back to my mother.

Following the truck, I missed the Mart cut off in Waco. I panicked. My mind whirled and then I heard, *"Now, Mom, you've taken this cut-off a hundred times in the last three months. You know how to go to the next exit and turn around. Good. Now swing around and follow the signs."* There was not a doubt in my mind that Debbie was making the trip home with me.

About ten miles from Mart I thought, how am I going to tell Mother? This trip could last forever, I thought, as I never wanted to get there. I'll just keep driving and driving into nowhere. But I did get there. After slowly pulling into the driveway, I got out of the car, still wondering how to handle the situation. I went next door to Sam and Alice and through fresh tears told them what had happened. They were stunned and wanted to come back over to the house with me. I must have looked like hell. I was in hell.

"No, not yet," I answered. "Give me a little while with Mother."

Entering the house, I realized Mother was asleep. Good, good, more time to think. So in my daze I walked the dogs. When I returned, I went into the bathroom, as I hadn't been since I'd left Mart at six o'clock. While I was in there Mom got up and came into the hallway.

"You're home so early?"

"Yes, I'll be done here in a second and then it's all yours."

I tried very hard for a normal voice. I listened to her go and then asked her to come into the bedroom. She sat on the edge of the bed and I sat next to her putting my arms around her.

"Mother, I have something to tell you. Our Debbie is gone." She looked at me, not understanding. Then it hit her and she jolted back, eyes wide. It registered. Then we both broke into a million pieces.

"I can't bear this," she mumbled.

"Yes, you can," I struggled to say. "We both have to somehow bear it because I need you to help me get through this. Right now I feel like I should go with her so she's not alone."

We both sat there rocking back and forth and finally got up and went into the living room. I sat in Debbie's chair, Mom sat on the sofa and that's where we stayed, rocking and crying, all night long, telling each other how we couldn't believe this had happened, over and over.

It wasn't yet light when I made us some coffee and walked the dogs, who'd been sleeping on Debbie's bed. Thoughts began to filter into my mind through the darkness. I was numb and unbelieving that our Debbie had been taken from us. Good God, not us. I had built the porch for us. I had been as prepared as I could for Mom passing, and Debbie and I had talked about what we were going to do when it happened. Get passports, take a trip, redo the house. But not this. I hadn't programmed this. Mother was supposed to have passed, not Debbie. I would now soon be alone. I was reeling. I'd had it all planned.

I couldn't even pray. I couldn't think; I couldn't function out of Debbie's chair. I wrapped her throw around me and sobbed.

Then something—or someone—took over and it was like I rose above myself and watched as I did all the things I had to do. I couldn't comprehend what was happening to me, but I knew it was time for me to let go and let God because I couldn't handle this anymore. I was helpless and mentally I was just slipping away into a dark place. To survive this horror I had to find relief. I had to be able to breathe. I had fallen into a deep pit. But God and my angels—Debbie's angels—were there to pick me up. I was not alone and never would be again.

Ten: How Do They Do That?

Some years ago I was sitting on the sofa reading, with the dog curled up beside me, when something dashed across the rug in front of the fireplace and disappeared. "What in the hell was that?" I asked out loud. The dog opened one eye, but didn't answer. The next day I was standing in front of the kitchen sink making a salad and something swished across my foot and—*poof*—was gone. I rose straight up off the floor, twisted around in mid-air, and came down on my ample butt on the counter top. A mouse! *I had a mouse!* Still reeling from a divorce, this was exactly what I did not need.

"What do I do about a mouse?" I asked my boss.

That night I went home armed with traps and cheddar cheese. After three days, I had to buy more cheese. Then I tried hot dogs and salami. No good.

"I'm going to have a four hundred pound gourmet mouse living in my kitchen cupboards," I wailed to co-workers. A week passed and I was fast coming to the realization that this mouse was smarter than me.

"Try peanut butter," suggested my boss.

Next night, *snap*. Then *snap* again. That meant two mice, deader than doornails.

But you know what? With all the mouse advice I'd gotten over the past week or so not one person told me that someone was going have to come with body bags to collect the remains. Nobody told me I was going to have to do this job myself.

That's where I stood that morning of October 30th. I had a job to do. A real mess to clean up. And I was a bigger mess. I was numb, flopping around, not believing that Debbie could possibly be gone from our lives. How could this have happened to me? It's not that she's gone; she's just not here at the moment, I told myself.

A driving force had settled deep inside me that blocked out what I could not accept, yet I knew I had to get about taking care of the living. So, like a bulldog, I set to work. It was again like I was watching my body function from some safe place because my mind was incapable of accepting. I moved like a robot, functioning on remote control. It would have been very easy not to speak to God any longer because I felt that the door to Him and Debbie had been slammed shut.

At six a.m. that morning I was at Clyde's Grocery buying the biggest trash bags in the largest box they had. Starting in the guest room, where Mom slept, I began pulling clothes from the closet, stripping it and the bureau. Debbie had been a compulsive eater and found relief from her emotions in food. She had clothes anywhere from a size fourteen to five

X, some with the tags still on where she had eaten herself out of one size and into another. Everything went into plastic bags and was dragged out into the living room. I was broken—not thinking—not aware. The only time I really lost control was when I found the Christmas presents she'd stuffed in the back of the closet. I knew one was mine because we'd talked about a scrap book for my plays, imagining pictures, playbills, reviews, et cetera, all in one place. Finding a starter scrapbook kit, I lost it.

By noon there were enough bags to fill the car. I made phone calls to family and friends but I couldn't talk much. I e-mailed Houston, "We've lost our beloved Debbie" and soon offers began to pour in. "We want to come to Mart right away to help." But I knew I had to do this alone. I had to lovingly go through everything and decide into what pile each item would go. And Debbie had been a packrat supreme. There had to be a pile for The Goodwill in Waco, a pile to go back with me to Houston, a pile for her dad, books to the library, the church food bank, the estate sale, and just plain junk. Mom and I made the first of many trips to the Waco Goodwill. They got to know us and what had happened. I knew we had to eat so we stopped and cried ourselves through a lunch. Then we loaded up empty boxes from Clyde's and stacked them in the carport for our "what goes where" piles. I continued to sleep on the sofa and did so until it was sold.

The hospital called the next day telling me that the University of Texas Medical Branch in Dallas had indeed accepted Debbie and would pick her up that afternoon. The papers had been faxed and I had to drive back to the hospital in Temple to sign them. When I pulled out of the hospital parking lot for the last time, I knew that Debbie's body was still inside and that it was my last chance to see her face again. Then a thought: *That's not so*. Mom and I drove back to Mart—destroyed. I would not allow myself to think about what was going to happen to Debbie's body. I only knew it was her wish to help future doctors learn and I'll never know what good would come out of it. They told me in a few weeks she would be cremated and her ashes sent to me in Houston. Everyone was extremely kind and as thoughtful as they could be under the circumstances, always stating that UT was very grateful for our sacrifice.

The next five days were a blur of frenzy. I made "ESTATE SALE – STARTING WEDNESDAY" signs and put them up all over town, priced everything to sell fast— translation: I was giving it away. I made a sign for the front of the house, "DEBBIE'S ESTATE SALE" so buyers couldn't miss the house.

On Monday, at ten a.m., TYC gave Debbie a beautiful memorial service which Mom and I attended. The cafeteria was filled with her co-workers remembering Debbie and her dedication to her kids. The director spoke of the hundreds of children that had passed through her hands during her career who were given a chance at rehabilitation and of their many success stories. These children had been removed from their homes for drug abuse, alcoholism, crimes against society, many to support their and sometimes their parent's habit. Everyone remembered the hours she put in, the time she took for each child, and the amount of her own money she spent on special occasions. She was acknowledged for the child who received a GED, a kid who walked away from a gang, the cakes she baked, the hugs, walks and talks, for a single piece of candy, but mostly it was her laugh. She had the greatest laugh in the world and it would ring down the hallways of this gray, walled and wired facility. They told me much later it was months before that laugher began to fade.

At this memorial service I was presented with a beautiful gift book in a carved wooden box. Everyone had signed and written notes to me in it and they slipped all her pictures inside. Her secretary had already brought me all her personal things from her office and I donated all her reference books to the school. They also had planned a memorial garden for her and placed a large oak bench there in her honor.

I don't know how I got back to the house. After the service, some of her co-workers came by and I gave them all remembrances. It was a beautiful and hellish day. I was proud that Debbie had done such a good job and was so loved. I was grateful I'd told her this when the flowers and cards began to arrive at the hospital. She had been so special to me and the world.

We went back to the house and I cleared out the bathroom and linen closet then took another carload to Goodwill.

One evening, Sam and Alice came by and sat me down at the kitchen table. "Alice and I have been talking about this," Sam said, "and we both agree. If you want, I'll buy this whole houseful of Debbie's things. Tell me how much you think it's all worth and I'll write you a check right now. That way you and Grandma can get back to Houston." I was floored. How generous of them. But we decided to wait until I'd had a chance to sell things on my own and see what was left at the end of the week.

Word spread around town like wildfire that there was this crazy woman disposing of a houseful of beautiful furnishings. The neighbors came. And then neighbors of the neighbors came. Then the relatives of the neighbors came. They came from near and far and they bought bags of linens, TV's, VCR, a new Gateway computer and everything that came with it, furniture, wall hangings and collections. The kitchen quickly cleaned out. What was left was tagged for pick up for the weekend. The house was half empty before the sale even started. When could we go home? Then a strong voice entered my mind, *"You'll be out of here by Saturday."*

There was another TYC offer. "Do you need any help?" This time, gratefully, "Yes. I need to get some of this stuff to Houston. I need someone to help me get me a trailer or a truck, get it loaded and drive it to my house because I only have room in my car for Mom, me, the dogs, and luggage.

"When do you want to leave?"

"Saturday morning." It was done.

Friday, I called the City of Temple regarding Debbie's death certificates. There was no funeral home to handle this and, as Debbie was sent to UT a lot of paperwork had to be done and signed by doctors and hospitals. It all took time.

"I have to leave for Houston on Saturday," I explained. "My mother is ninety-two and has Alzheimer's. I have to get her home."

"Come to the office here in Temple and pay for the certificates and we'll mail them to you."

There was just time for one last Waco Goodwill trip. The house was cleaned out. I then drove to Temple, past the dreaded hospital, to City Hall. I ordered twelve certified certificates, paid for them, and got the hell out of there. When I got back to Mart, I cancelled all the utilities and TV services. They were disconnected as of November 15th, the final bills to be sent to me.

Saturday morning, Alex Watts and I went and got the trailer. Two of Debbie's co-workers were there when we got back and the trailer was loaded in twenty minutes. Whatever few things were left in the kitchen or the house I gave to them. All her outdoor plants went to the Sam and Alice. Mom and I got in the car, took a last look at Debbie's little house, and said goodbye to Mart, Texas forever.

I've always heard people say that they didn't know how they picked out a loved one's clothes or flowers, a casket for burial, and coped with the endless, heartless paperwork. They wondered how they ever got through it all. How? I really didn't know myself then, but I do now. Angels do it for you.

Eleven: Home & The Great Funk

Home was like a great empty cave, cold and unwelcoming. I got in my recliner, turned on the TV, and stayed there for days at a time, doing only what I needed to do to take care of Mom, the house, and the dogs. I slept a lot, but I couldn't read or write. I woke up in the morning and for a few seconds everything was great. I'd move around in the bed stretching, testing how good my back was going to be that day, wondering what the weather was like outside, and then—*wham*— I'd remember and would be gripped with a gut-wrenching physical pain that took my breath away, the kind of pain that will make you groan out loud in agony. My soul hurt, my body hurt, but my mind said, "*Get up, get up, move, move.*"

So I did, but I was shaky, my mind slipping in and out of reality. Going to the grocery store was torture. I found myself putting things Debbie liked in the basket because she'd be home in a week or so and she'd really enjoy this or that. It was a beautiful November and we could maybe have lunch on the porch. Then I'd remember and put the items back on the shelves, screaming inside, as the tears ran down my face.

I cried myself sick, privately, so as not to upset Mom. I had no idea how much Mom had taken in as she would say things at times to me like, "Well, I'll just go to Debbie's if you want to go to Austin for that conference." She was a long way from the woman who a few years before driven an RV across the country and mowed down most of the mailboxes on her street.

Then, suddenly, it was Thanksgiving. My friend Caroline called. She and another friend, Louella, were cooking Thanksgiving dinner and wanted Mom and I to come, just the four of us. Good food, good wine, and good friends. It was a quiet dinner where we laughed and cried and had a lot of wine. Caroline was going to Ireland for Christmas. Her daughter had married an Irish lad and they were all going to Dublin for an Irish Christmas. I'd brought her Debbie's new luggage. It had made only one trip to New York that summer so she could visit her dad, Caroline had been on her way out the door to shop for new luggage when I called her from Mart.

"Would you like this luggage for your trip?"

"Absolutely," she answered.

"Good. I'll pack all three pieces full of things I want to bring home and then they're yours."

And that's what we did. Caroline got the luggage and Mom and I got a dinner and an evening at the theater. It was a terrific deal.

The next night Mom and I went to see *DIVA* at Stages Theatre. I think it was really good but I'm not sure. But I was up and out of that recliner with a voice in my head urging me to stay up. *Get busy. Stay busy. Do what you have to do. You are not finished by a long way.*

Debbie's car was still parked in my driveway and I had a garage full of boxes and beautiful artwork. Okay, I bargained with myself, one box a day. And that's all I could handle. The Saturday morning after Thanksgiving I took a cup of coffee out to the garage and just looked around. Then, later, I sort of shoved a few boxes around and stacked the artwork. I started to think about the things I had packed in those boxes that were Debbie's: my mother's china, her stemware, and her silver. There were boxes of household paper goods, cleaners, shampoo, un-opened make up, two boxes to go to her dad, computer supplies, picture albums, and jewelry. I couldn't even remember all the items I had brought home, but one thing I knew for sure: I had to make room for this stuff and that meant I had to pack up a lot of my things. That was enough thinking for that day.

The next day I started to work. Finding boxes, I packed up all my china and stemware in order to replace it with Mom's. I went through cupboards, storage shelves, tops of closets, and the pantry. Out went my old spices—and I mean old. I loaded up boxes of old cookware, plastic storage containers—with and without lids—cookie cutters, whatever I hadn't used in the last year went into a box. It was like I was moving. Out with the old and in with the new. Only it wasn't new—it was Debbie's life. And it was done one box at a time.

I'd hung some of her artwork in various rooms in the house. Pictures of Galveston's historic homes and I remembered the summers we rented a beach house, the Christmas we spent at a haunted B&B on 18th Street and, after a few stories from our host, Debbie ending up in bed with Mom and me. The Saturday we spent at *Dickens On The Strand* and, while walking a gray, windblown beach, found nestled in the seaweed a barnacle covered bottle with a note in it. Carefully removing the note, which was written in English, and drying it out it informed us a man in Mexico had set three bottles adrift a few months ago just to see what would happen. He included his name and phone number and, of course, Debbie called him that night. We were all excited over our adventure and it was written up in the Galveston paper. The bottle and note sit in my study to this day.

***

The death certificates finally arrived. Now the business end started. Sending letters, I closed charge accounts, canceled her car insurance, sent notes to doctors and hospitals informing them of Debbie's passing and enclosed a certified copy of her death certificate. I paid her final bills and closed her bank accounts. TYC needed a copy of the death certificate to apply for her life insurance. Soon I would have to clean out her car and sell it. On and on it went.

That's how the next few weeks passed. I was determined to block out Christmas. It was our time of year. We'd always had a big Christmas and started putting away presents as early as August. It always took Mom and me three days to decorate—and we loved it. We both wanted the house to look like Christmas when Debbie got home: the tree glowing, the mantle shining, the Christmas village, where battery operated street lights blinked and ice skaters made their figure eights. There were only a few Christmas holidays she missed coming home because of her job. With years of seniority, she'd made a deal with co-workers. "You can have Thanksgiving and New Year's," Debbie had always said, "But Christmas is mine."

Not this year. I attempted a couple of Christmas parties but we left with tears streaming down my face.

Mom and I only wanted to be alone. I hated the phone to ring because it wasn't Debbie calling. I didn't want to talk to anyone else and was hardly civil. We didn't want to visit with anyone or go anywhere. I was in a deep, dark, hole and I pulled it up over my head. We went to Paul and Katherine's for Christmas dinner—a brave front.

Not a card was mailed nor a string of tinsel hung. Mom and I did not exchange gifts. We hardly talked. The pain was unbelievable as New Year's came and went. Thank God, the holidays were over. There was nothing to pack away, no leftovers, no hangovers, no nothing. Just a sad house, a packed garage, and a life full of memories.

I mailed two boxes of Debbie's personal items to her dad in New York, hung a few more of her pictures, and then said a thankful goodbye to 2007.

Twelve: That's One

Most of us know the story of the old farmer who'd just gotten married and he was driving his new bride, in his horse and wagon, to her new home. Ambling along, the horse stumbles jolting the wagon, and the farmer says firmly, "That's one." A little further down the road the horse clops to the side of the road to munch some grass. "That's two," says the farmer sternly, jerking up the horse's head. At the farm gate the horse suddenly decides he wants no part of it and sits down. "That's three," roars the farmer, as he gets down, takes a 2x4 out of the back of the wagon and whacks the horse a good one on the rump. "Oh, you beast," screeches the new wife, "How can you treat your poor horse like that? Have I married a man of no compassion?" Looking up, the farmer says, "That's one."

On January 8, 2008, I not only got my first "That's One," I got the full whack.

Only this one was to the side of my head—*wham!* I had to take Mom to her regular check up at the doctors at eleven a.m. that day. It was really important I didn't miss this one because, after what we'd been through, I wanted her checked over. Dr. Cleaver knew about our loss as I had been in for a sore mouth a few weeks before. "Am I at the wrong doctor?" I asked. "Should I be seeing a dentist?"

"Nope," he answered. "This is stress." And he gave me a prescription for a mouth salve and asked me if I needed a little something to take the edge off. Then I'd have two problems, I told him, instead of one. I'd still have to get through the grief and then have to kick the pills – no thanks. He just looked at me over his glasses and I went on about my miserable way to clean out Debbie's car as I had sold it.

I left early for Mom's appointment as I wanted to stop by the Social Security office with a copy of Debbie's death certificate to make sure her Social Security number was closed out and couldn't be used by anyone. Even at nine a.m. the office was crowded, and instead of being rushed through with what I thought was something minor, I had to take a number and wait it out. My number was forty-eight. I finally got Mother a seat across from me and continued to wait, fidgeting and sighing, although the system was moving along pretty fast. At about number forty I pulled out the death certificate and, for lack of something else to do, I looked it over again. Numbers forty-one and forty-two were called. There were people seated all around me: a large African-American man was quietly reading beside me, a Spanish woman was trying in vain to rein in her three kids, and there were many troubled retirees deep in their own thoughts.

Now, I'd handled this death certificate many times in the past weeks while processing Debbie's paperwork but now something caught my eye I hadn't seen before. There was a small box to the right of the certificate and in small letters it read, "Time of Death: 18:20. I'd noticed the 18:20 before but thought it was some sort of code because, as usual, I probably didn't have my glasses on and couldn't have read the tiny "Time of Death" portion. For some reason, and for the first time, I realized it must be military time. Counting it out on my fingers; 18:20 was – let's see now – twelve o'clock, one o'clock, two o'clock, so 18:20 was actually – six-twenty p.m. The ceiling fell in on me, I remembered Debbie's doctor saying "come right away," the rush to Temple, the turn signal suddenly gone crazy, the voice in my mind screaming, *"Look at the clock, the clock on the dash. This is important."* It hit me like a truck. Debbie had passed at six- twenty p.m., the exact time the left hand turn signal in my car had started wildly blinking and I had known in my soul that something was very wrong.

My hands began to shake and I knew the color had drained from my face. I tried to get Mother's attention but couldn't speak or move. Then quite softly the man who had been reading beside me said, "Excuse me, but would it be all right if I gave you a Bible verse?" I could only nod as he reached in his pocket and handed me a small card with the verse printed on it. I know I put it in my pocket and then heard, "Number forty-eight." I somehow got up and walked the ten steps or so to the window. Then I turned back to look for the man who had been sitting beside me moments before, the black man who had given me the Bible verse – but he was gone.

I quickly did my business, collected Mother and got out of there as fast as I could. She had no idea what had just happened and I don't remember if I told her at that time, but I did get her to the doctor's for her appointment. Two minutes after he entered the examination room, I went to pieces. Poor Dr. Cleaver sat on his stool while I, sobbing and raving like a lunatic, tried to tell him about the turn signal, the time on the death certificate, and the man with the Bible verse. I suddenly realized he and my mother were looking at me in a strange way. I took a deep breath and shut up before they made arrangements to lock me up someplace bleak and sad.

"I think you need a little something," he said, reaching for his prescription pad.

"No. I'm fine," I gulped. "It was just a shock. I'll be okay."

He examined Mom and told me she was doing well. By then I had dragged myself somewhat together. "I still think you need a prescription to help to settle you down," he said as we left the examination room, his arm around me. I did. But the help I needed didn't come in a bottle.

The next day, January 9th, I headed for the garage. Cleaning out Debbie's car, I'd found her holistic cache: her tarot cards, palm reading books, angel kits and cards, holistic literature, and a heart shaped rose crystal. I'd packed them all in a box to give to her cousin. Now I hauled it into the house. I ran my fingers over her Angel Therapy Kit, finally opening it. I set up the board and read the directions. Before long I was throwing the dice and asking questions.

(Q) Is Debbie an angel? (A) No.

(Q) Is she my guardian angel? (A) Doubtful.

(Q) Is she in heaven watching over me? (A) Of course.

That was it. I couldn't take anymore. I put the kit away. But deep down I knew the truth. I remembered John Edward saying at the beginning of his *Cross Country* show. "How do I know? I just do." Debbie had come to say goodbye and I had met my first Bible verse-toting angel at the Social Security office.

"And ye shall seek me, and find me and
ye shall search for me with all your heart."
Jeremiah 29:13

Thirteen: Are You Talkin' To Me?

Nothing had changed. The same ol' crap the next morning: waking up, suddenly remembering my reality, and then the hammer hits you in the stomach. I knew I had to get some relief from this deep, dark pain. Good God, I couldn't be the only one suffering like this from the loss of a child. I dragged out the Angel Therapy Kit and started asking questions. I hardly knew how to use the board or what to ask but I'd already stuck my toe in the water.

(Q) Do I have angels around me? (A) Yes.

(Q) Do I have a guardian angel? (A) Yes.

The board had twelve categories so I branched out.

(Q) How do I get some relief from this pain? (A) Surrender and Release.

(Q) Where do I go from here? (A) Search.

Search? Okay, I get it. If I was going to get through this I was going to have to search and ask for help. I did. Now, prayer and meditation had never been a daily activity for me but I tried. I got quiet, took a few deep breaths and asked God for his help. I asked him to send me some of Debbie's angels to help me find my way. I remembered Debbie saying, "Don't worry, Mom, my angels are all around me."

Prayer was very informal. I just got in there and asked for relief and got out. I tried to meditate by getting myself comfortable and quiet but all I did was cry and I just couldn't settle down.

There was only one place I knew about that would understand what was happening to me and that was Unity Church. Years ago, when my second marriage was starting to leak, I thought maybe we needed some religious grounding. I was raised a Methodist and he, a Baptist. When we married we joined a Baptist church close to the house. My dad had passed the year before and my mother was visiting us from Florida at the time and when I told her I was going to be baptized the following Sunday, she asked, "What's the matter, didn't the first one take?" Apparently not, and this one didn't either. My only thought during the service was "lunch." I was talking to a friend of mine about it one day and she suggested we try Unity Church. We did and we liked it. It was called "The Pyramid" because that's exactly what it was. A huge, golden pyramid set back on Unity Drive. The sanctuary was quiet, peaceful and smelled of fresh cedar. I learned to meditate, sing the Peace Song, and, being the eternal controller that I am, tried to let go of a wayward husband and let God deal with it all. I dipped into new ideas. Life after death, past lives, reincarnation, healing, loving yourself, that was a leap for me, to stop whining and get on with it. Help is there for you if you ask for it.

Next thing I knew I was being asked for a divorce. There was someone else. I cried, begged, and watched him pack up and go. Debbie came home for a few days and Mother came for a month. I called Silent Unity for someone—anyone—to pray for me. In shock, I painted the back bedroom and then I withdrew from the world.

A year later I had a good job and had learned to live alone. Debbie was out of college and starting her career and Mom was back in Florida doing crafts and pool aerobics with about one hundred other retired white haired widows.

I decided I really wasn't cut out to spend my life on a bar stool, which was where I was spending a lot of time, so I went back to school and started writing.

About that time Debbie and her college roommate, Hope, went to Europe. Hope's sister was teaching for the military in Germany and they made Hamburg their home base and branched out from there. They loved Germany and rode Eurail like pros, visiting Italy, France, and hitting England on the way home. Hope's sister went along with them when she could. They stayed in guest homes, picnicked out of the local markets, and laughed their way across the continent. They must have been a charming trio of rascals and had not one unpleasant encounter, unless you want to count the German fellow they met in a café that was insistent he must marry Debbie. They were gone a month and came home with wonderful stories, memories, and red hot American Express cards. I asked her what impressed her most on her trip and she promptly answered, "Dachau." Debbie was half Jewish.

So Mom was in Florida, Debbie had her own life, and I was lonely and needed company. Unity Church drew me back. I returned and joined Unity Singles and made a lot of friends. There was always something to do: a meeting during the week, a weekend movie or house party—lots of house parties. The word was out: if you want to meet a hot-to-trot divorcee, check out the church singles groups. Then one Sunday morning, as we all gathered on the patio for coffee before the service, contemplating the big question of the day—which restaurant was offering free champagne for Sunday brunch that day?— I spotted him: my ex-husband and his new wife just across the patio, smiling and greeting old friends. I never went back.

***

Now, I pulled Unity Church up on the computer. It was still there and still across town from me. I looked again. There was another Unity Church in Northwest Houston. A new one and close to me. Mom and I drove over to check it out. It was a lovely, smaller church tucked into the woods. We went inside to look around. There were silver and gold angels in the lobby. The sanctuary was cool and quiet with small angels placed about the pulpit and in wall hangings. A huge white dove, in flight, seemed to move across the cedar cross. I knew I was home.

Back at the computer and pulled up "grief" and there it was, Compassionate Friends. They met once a month and they had a meeting not far from my house that very night.

"Do you want to go to this meeting with me tonight?" I asked Mom.

"Do you think it will help?"

"I don't know, but we can't be alone in this. Lots of people have lost children."

"Not like Debbie."

Mom and I went and I found out that we were certainly not the only ones grieving over the loss of a child.

I literally crawled into that meeting, my eyes almost swollen shut from crying. My mother had been wringing her hands over what to do with me. What did she do with her grief? How did she handle it? Debbie was the light of her life. She once told me she did her crying at night. I was really too deep in my own anguish to care. Anyway, there was coffee and snacks and lots of Kleenex. I couldn't talk, so I just listened. I listened to the stories: the car wrecks, motor cycle accidents, the medication accidents, the suicides, the overdoses, and the cancers. It was mostly women that night and all of us crying for each other. As the death stories continued around the large conference table I heard, "I lost my Dillon three years ago March." "I lost Adrian five years ago. He was twenty-two." "My Susan was in a car wreck with three of her friends two years ago this May. She was seventeen and the only one that died."

All I was hearing was two years ago, five years ago, and seven years ago. My God, I thought, I can't stand this now so how will I ever last for years? I didn't know as another mother told how hard it was for her to go to the grocery store, another that she flies out of her skin when the phone rings still thinking it's her son calling her, and I knew I was in the right place and I'd be back.

"Do you want to go with me again next month?"

"Yep," was her answer.

***

On January 12th I finally talked with Pam, Debbie's cousin, and told her about the incident in the car and that I was convinced that it was Debbie saying goodbye. "I really want to hear about this," she said, "but I have to go now. I'll call you back."

Sure.

But she did. And she agreed it was a "bye, Mom" from Debs.

I kept going back to meditation, closing my eyes and trying hard to concentrate on nothing when that day, two things happened. The first, a thought: *keep a journal*. And the second: through the darkness I began to see a swirling haze that was a light gray color. The haze began to look like clouds and these clouds slowly circled around behind my eyes. I wasn't afraid but it was a little unnerving.

The next Sunday in church during meditation, my gray swirling clouds began to get some color. What's going on now, I thought. They just moved around slowly and in and out of each other, joining colors and then moving on. It was rather restful and I began to enjoy the quietness and peace they brought.

I went to a used bookstore and bought *Spirit Guides & Angels* by Richard Webster, *Meet & Work With Spirit Guides* by Ted Andrews, and *Crystal Healing* by Phyllis Galde. In my church bookstore I was tripping over angles, books, figurines, tapes, and crystals. I couldn't get enough "angel" information. I went on the net and read about all the archangels and matched them with the books I was reading.

***

I was still crying a lot and completely losing it at times but I was beginning to be able to breathe, being a little calmer, and found myself not being so impatient with Mom. I was communicating easier with her and friends instead of locking myself up. But I would still wander around my house looking at Debbie's things, all the gifts she'd given me over the years, and I could not believe she was gone. I could not talk about her yet, and if anyone mentioned her to me I was destroyed on the spot. It seemed my grief was all I had left of her. Could I find an antidote to my grief in books? Hell if I knew.

I was still asking my questions to the Angel Therapy Kit but now I was making notes of my answers. I was burning through any New Age books I could find, learning about angels, after death experiences, what authors thought heaven was like. Then one day I discovered that the television show *John Edward Cross Country* was not Senator John Edwards traveling around giving political speeches. I'd passed on this program several times thinking just that. I couldn't believe what I was seeing and hearing. There was John in his sweater and jeans passing on messages from the other side to relatives and friends on this side. Right there, in his studio. And they were crying and I was crying. What kind of crap is this? But the next day I watched it again, then ordered two of his and a couple of Shirley MacLaine's books.

***

I was eating again, just a little, and sleeping a little better. You'd have thought I would have lost a ton of weight. I know I did by some of my clothes, but nothing dramatic, but I still shut myself off from the world. I took care of Mom, the dogs, got a haircut when I needed it, but mostly I just read, prayed for help getting through this, meditated, watched my colored clouds float around, checked my e-mail, ordered more books from Amazon.com, watched endless TV, threw my dice, and asked my questions.

(Q) Are angles always around me? (A) Definitely
(Q) Is Gabriel guiding my creativity? (A) Yes
(Q) What will further my spirituality? (A) An Open Heart
(Q) Are all my passed relatives spirit guides? (A) No
(Q) Are my clouds spirit energy? (A) Yes
(Q) Will I ever be able to let go of control? (A) Soon

***

That afternoon I went to the grocery store and bought Mom and myself two California navel oranges. The next day I went to get one to cut up for lunch and there was only one orange in the fridge. Taking the keys, I went out to check the trunk and, sure enough, there was the stray orange wedged up against the back seat. I got it out and stuck it in the fridge so it would be cold for the next day. Next morning I couldn't find my car keys. Frantically, I tore up the house looking for them. Not only were the car keys on that ring, but the house keys, the garage door key, and the keys to open the burglar bars. Again, I searched the house but no luck. Beaten, I slumped down in my chair and said, "Okay, angels, I give up. If you want 'em, you got 'em. Just show me what to do now." I relaxed for a while, meditated, and watched my colored clouds swirl around my head. Then one of the purple ones was suddenly orange and passed by very quickly. It was just a flash. Then a thought: *"check the car"*. I went out and from the dash opened the trunk and there were my keys. I'd dropped them when I'd gone orange fishing.

Give it up for the angels.

Fourteen: Say Goodbye To January

The month of January was winding down and I was feeling better, eating a little more, and doing what had to be done. Friends were calling me and trying their best to get me interested in *something*. Of course, I was floating off in the world of angels, meditations, swirling colored clouds, and whatever. I was feeling spacey and finally realized I needed something to ground me, so I went to a meeting at Scriptwriters/Houston and then out to eat with the gang.

Horacio called and wanted me to read my new ten minute play, *What?* for a Valentine's Day party he was throwing. Pulling it out, I started the rewrite, then started work on a new ten-minute play, *Feng Shui*. It was mostly just to see if I could concentrate on a story line. It was a hard go as I could barely focus on a page or two of recreational reading, except for books on angels and metaphysical topics, let alone a blank computer page, but I was writing again. Not good and not fast, but doing it.

That weekend I saw Paul Young's new play at Theatre One and submitted a couple of my older plays into competition. As time went on, I found myself reading more and more: Shirley MacLaine's *Out On A Limb* and *The Camino*, then another book on spirit guides. Since I'd been busy reading I'd noticed a lot less bubble ups. But, Debbie, bless her, still appeared briefly in my dreams.

***

I called Pam, Debbie's cousin, one day late in the month and we talked about her brother and his girlfriend who'd driven to New York last year for a wedding. The second day of the trip they were hit by another car and forced off the road. The car burst into flames; both were burned beyond recognition. This had happened the previous summer and Debbie, Mom and I had gone to the funeral. Pam and I were talking about strange things happening and she said that for weeks before the accident she had smelled smoke. She'd commented on it to the family but no one else noticed a smoky odor.

Later in the day, I made a trip to the post office to mail off some play scripts as I had pulled *Ralph and Cleo's Crazy Christmas*, a children's play, out of a file and was sending out copies to four publishers. I'd been doing a lot of angel card readings and they kept coming up *Submit* and *Now's the time.*

It was like I was possessed to keep busy—on a treadmill, not allowing my mind to drift to the loss of Debbie. It was still very hard. I missed her so much I ached and most of the time I still couldn't believe this had happened. It was like a bad dream. I was still crying miserably as January came to a close.

What was I doing? I asked myself. I still hurt so bad I felt my chest was crushed. *"Get up and get going,"* my mind told me. *"You can't think about two things at once."* My turning to prayer and meditation sometimes twice a day kept me calmer and it was beginning to get easier. I started taking Mom to plays and movies and out of the house every day, even if it was just for a short drive. We were even doing a light lunch out now and then, since both of us were beginning to eat again. We were actually going out into the sunshine, going to church and tithing, going to Compassionate Friends, visiting an AARP nursing home once a month. Still, I felt restless and unsure, but I'd sworn I'd do anything to relieve this pain. Whenever thoughts of the hospitals, the commutes, Debbie's surgeries, or her cute little house crept in, I'd let them wash over me and then try to chase them away. I wanted to scream, "don't go there, don't go there." It's painful there. But I had to go. It was Debbie.

I was reading like a fiend now as it was an escape from my own thoughts. Near the end of the month I got up early and walked the dogs a long way. While walking, I had a sudden vision of Debbie laid out on a table. "What's that about?" I asked out loud. And then I remembered. January 29th, it had been three months since Debbie's passing. When I got home I called on my support and healing angels. I was in a bucket of it today and I knew it. I started a new short play—anything to move out of my thoughts. I started making plans for the reading of *What?* My dear friend, Eddie, called to encourage me to submit *The Last Posse* to the McLaren Comedy Competition. I did it.

January 31, my birthday, came and went on a breath of air. No flowers, no card or call from Debbie. I went to visit the nursing home for a few hours. Now, there's something that will really cheer you up!

Fifteen: Finding A Way

February is the beginning of spring in Texas. Wild flowers and bulbs are beginning to poke up here and there. Although you're saying to yourself, "Too early, guys; at least two more good freezes before Easter," I've been fooled more than once when warm spring breezes and a temperate sun sends me to the local nursery and I spend the weekend planting my prizes and the next covering them up.

Eldridge Publishing sent back *Capote Tonight* as being too adult for them but wanted to see what else I had. They liked my style. I sent them a few synopsis, but suddenly felt fear. But fear of what, I wondered? I was so thankful that God and my angels were beginning to find me things to do and to take an interest in that I had forgotten about other feelings. Grief no longer ruled my life. Now panic was creeping in and settling in my gut. I sat down and meditated, asking God to allow the Archangel Michael to remove this fear and replace it with some of his strength and courage. I realized that I'd always feared success, maybe more than disappointment. I told people I took rejection well and now was not the time for such deep concerns. I had a lot to do.

One was filing Debbie's final tax return. I asked for a lot of help with that one as I had to go through all her papers and I didn't handle it very well. My mind kept bouncing around—even meditation didn't quiet me down. Somehow I got the damned tax information together for my accountant and then buried myself in *Out On A Limb* by Shirley MacLaine.

This was my second reading, the first done years ago, and suddenly memories flooded into my mind as I read and drifted off in thought to my second husband, Jim, and our exploring Unity Church for the first time and liking it. Then Unity Singles after the inevitable divorce, enrolling in Houston Community College and taking writing courses from Professor Diana Birch, Diana, who was writing her 18th century novel. Diana and her cerebral affair with the Duke of Rochester; later convinced she was carrying his child. Diana, taking me to a channeler who told me to get rid of my anger—and that someone, a male, was writing through me.

I remembered Mom sitting next to me in church years ago and during a meditation suddenly turning to me and saying, "I just had a visit from your Grandmother and she said not to be afraid, everything was fine." My mother who thought microwaves were spooky.

I had a lot of memories.

I wasn't a newcomer to metaphysics or the New Age. We had a history, but it was thirty years ago. There'd been questions about my first play, *Amigos,* based on the dirty war in Argentina. When a University of Houston researcher looked it over, she asked, "How did you know about some of this material?"

"Beats me. It was just there."

"How much research did you do?"

"I did absolutely none."

"Interesting," she replied. She and her partner belonged to Unity Church. That's where we met.

Continuing to meditate I drifted on, seeing animal totems and realizing I had always had something going with animals. I couldn't stand for an animal to be mistreated. I took in strays and loved them unconditionally. I couldn't watch a TV program or a movie where animal cruelty was depicted. They were once rounding up wild mustangs in West Texas and it was on the news. Apparently, there were so many mustangs they were starving and some had to be destroyed. It really upset me. My mom said, "If we got one, we'd have to get a bigger dog door as it would have free rein of the house and would probably sleep in your bed." No doubt about it.

Back into my meditation, the colors were blue, purple, and gold, swirling like a lava lamp, then a flash of cobalt blue before they were gone.

Debbie had inherited my love of animals. Silky, her black cocker spaniel, was the love of her life. When she lived at the lake house, all the dogs in the neighborhood found their way to her door and the giant bag of dog food she always kept handy. Once, one of these dogs came calling and he just didn't look right to Debbie. He came around again later and it was the same story, no one seemed to be around to take care of this animal. Debbie put him into her car and took him to her vet. It wasn't good. The dog had distemper and nothing could be done. She asked the vet to put him down and paid for it. Then all hell broke loose. The owners showed up and had a "you killed our dog" fit and poor Debbie almost had to move to Seattle to avoid the backlash. It finally calmed down but she swore she'd never get involved in a situation like that again.

That night I dreamed of Debbie. She was in her room with a friend, and I hurried in to tell her a terrible mistake had been made, because everyone thought she was dead. I hugged her, crying in relief, and woke up. Wiping tears, I dressed and prepared *Capote Tonight* to be submitted to Theatre Lab, in Houston; *Pages* went to McLaren, in Midland, Texas.

That week I went to a Scriptwriter's meeting and listened to a reading of a short play in progress. It was about a guy who came back from the dead. I turned to my friend George and asked, "Do you believe in reincarnation?" He looked surprised, and answered with a question. "Do you?" I confessed to him that I had been reading a lot of metaphysical books and that I was particularly interested in angels. "Well, if you see any, let me know," he said. He had just had open heart surgery and was going through a divorce. He needed an angel or two.

Mom was doing pretty well, but she didn't talk about Debbie much. That was okay with me, since we always cried, and what good did that do? One evening at Compassionate Friends I was quietly listening to some of their stories and hearing a mother tell of her worry about crying so much, when I blurted out, "I don't know why I cry. Is it because I miss Debbie so much or because I miss our codependent relationship? Maybe I cry for myself." It got real quiet. I remember reading that the disciples cried when Jesus said He was ascending to the Father. He knew He was going to a glorious place and so did his disciples. They couldn't follow Him yet; maybe that's why they cried. Maybe that's why I cry.

***

I kept reading about angels and one day Mother asked me, "Where are all these angels and spirits you're always reading about?"

"They're all around us. They're with us all the time."

"I thought so" she replied. And that was the end of our conversation.

The next day Mom and I had dentist appointments. Right in the middle of my examination I started to cry. Huge silent tears ran down my cheeks from under the safety glasses and when I looked down I could see my chest quivering under the wrap.

"Am I hurting you?" he asked, concerned.

"No, no. I'm okay. Don't pay any attention."

"She just lost her daughter a while ago," volunteered his assistant, as she probed my mouth with the water sucker.

He patted my shoulder and we got the job done, but when we were finished I looked a mess—all red faced and frog-eyed. I told him how embarrassed I was.

"I have to go through your waiting room looking like this," I wailed. "All your patients will think you were killing me in here." We were both laughing by then. Later that night he called my house to see if I was all right. I assured him I was. Wow! When was the last time your dentist called you to see if you were all right?

Then I developed a new trick. I got cold. Not just chilly where you'd have to put on a sweater, but a bone-chilling cold where you had to get into a hot bath to thaw out then wrap yourself in quilts until you stopped shaking. This happened without warning. I'd usually fall asleep before I warmed up.

One day, buried beneath my quilt, I fell asleep and had a dream. I was talking to a young girl and suddenly realized it was Debbie! I got very emotional and told her how much I loved her and missed her and asked if she could stay with me now. She told me she could. Then my mother walked in the room and I said, "Look, Debbie's home," and Mother fainted dead away. We got her on her feet and she took another look at Debbie and she went down again. "She's gone out again," I said. Suddenly there were other people around helping me with her and I woke up, only this time saying "Thank you, God" for my visit.

I was having a productive period. I hoped it would last. That Monday night I attended a Scriptwriter's meeting and got into it with a couple of brain dead members. These two had definite opinions regarding homosexuality and insulted a good friend of mine and his partner at the meeting. My friend was so mortified he left and I came apart. To make it worse the next day I tore them up again on the phone to another friend of mine, yada, yada, yada. I'll do better tomorrow, I promised myself.

The very next morning I yelled at Mom for endlessly feeding the dogs people cookies. Every two days I was filling up the cookie jar. The dogs were getting so fat they were about to explode. I knew she was giving them cookies because every time she goes into the kitchen both dogs would drag themselves up from their naps and faithfully follow her into the food chamber. I explained to her that people cookies are not good for the dogs, and that they have their own sugar free cookies. "Do not do this," I said. But, as Henry Higgins says, "She listens very nicely and then does precisely what she wants."

***

The first of Debbie's insurance money arrived the next day. I looked at that check and asked myself what part of her was worth this amount. I was still harboring a hollow, deep sadness. I missed her so much that there were times I was convinced it was all a bad dream. I felt helpless.

Then my out-of-this-world Mother wouldn't let me wash her hair that morning. Crap, I thought, and let it go. I felt tired and cold in spite of the beautiful, warm, spring day. It was a new season and I felt like I was frittering away my days. I've got to get off my ass and do something, I thought; the something I felt I was being led to, if I could only figure out what it was. I'd read something interesting that day in one of my angel books: not only do angels have names but they have colors: Gabriel, copper; Raphael, emerald green; Raquel, light pink; Uriel, amber; and Michael; blue and purple. Well, now I knew where my colored clouds came from. Thank you, my friends.

***

I went to another meeting of Compassionate Friends. It was a big meeting and there were fathers there this time, looking as if they had taken a beating. They had. All the seats were filled. I took Mom, but it was a losing battle. There was the eternal sighing, the drumming on the table, and then falling asleep. I'd have to get someone to stay with her, as it was too much for her to be out that late at night. That week I found a sitter for Mother.

The meeting started and the stories began. The group leader, a man, lost his son eleven years ago and still broke down in telling his story. The other two men came with their wives and by the time they finished telling their stories we were all in tears. One had lost his fourteen year old son in an auto accident; the other, a seven year old, to cancer. We went around the room but I still couldn't talk about Debbie's death so I told them about our family trip to Cancun: It was August, and hotter than hell. Our hotel was right on the beach and the blue surf swept right up to the shore where beach chairs and umbrellas were lined up like brightly painted ducks. There was a cabana boy selling souvenirs, struggling with his load, and calling out, "Cheap today." From then on everything we saw was "cheap today" for us. The water was like velvet and, with Mom holding our suits in waist high surf, Debbie and I went skinny dipping at night. We learned to sail a Sunfish, went on a pirate ship to an island for lunch and snorkeling, her holding my hand underwater until I got used to it. Then we took a sweltering bus ride to Chichen Itza, the Mayan ruins, and ate ice cold mangos on a stick. I got through it and it was a good thing.

The pain in that room was stifling. There were tales of lots of auto and motorcycle accidents, a suicide, and drug overdoses. We talked about everyday things: How hard it was to do familiar chores—cleaning their rooms, touching their things, grocery shopping and not buying their favorite foods. One woman talked about having to pull the plug on her daughter and I thought, Thank you, God, I didn't have to do that. Another sits for hours beside her daughter's grave, writing to her in a journal.

We talked about the strange things that were happening to us, about visitation dreams—one man shared how he had a dream about his passed son. He'd called his wife, who was in Germany at the time, and she'd had the same dream. Another mother praying in a cemetery saying out loud, "Show me a sign," and a bell, hanging from a tree, rang in the distance. Another went to a memorial for deceased children sponsored by Compassionate Friends and they sent up balloons with a personal message attached. Up they went, between twenty to thirty brightly colored balloons into a soft blue cloudless sky. When she got to her car, there was her balloon by the car door with her message still attached. This is the same woman who sleeps all night on her sofa which faces the front door. Her son always wanted something to eat when he came in late. She's still waiting for him.

We talked about the changes in us. Our loss of memory, that there were proven chemical changes a shock like this makes on the brain, fear of things you never thought about before, loss of appetite, not being able to concentrate on anything for long, being able to read no more than a couple of pages at a time.

The facilitator said that nothing would ever be the same again; we had to find a new normal. The pain we're suffering keeps our loved one's spirit close. In order to get on with your physical lives, we have to let go of this pain and allow our love ones to get on with their spiritual ones. What's this? Physical life and spiritual life?

And that's when I got it. Debbie may not be here in the physical, but she's sure here in the spiritual. She's all around me every day, helping me with her "Okay, Mom." I had found the right place. I was not alone. None of us were.

***

Valentine's Day came and went in sweet, tearful memories. In the prior few years neither Debbie nor I had much of a love life so we sent each other little things enclosed in Valentine cards, things like a silly pencil or a new magnet for the refrigerator, anything that would make us laugh. That year I bought Mom a box of candy and called it a day.

I'd found a new angel book and whipped through it. I read that when you have an angel encounter the experience changes you drastically. I agreed. I was changing. My interests were different, my outlook was turning around, my compassion for friends went up a notch, my fears were subsiding—and when they overtook me I knew where to go for relief. I found myself opening to opportunity like never before, instead of closing down with the thought that someone just wants something from me and to hell with them. Could I possibly come out of this a new person, a re-born person? Where had I read that to enter the kingdom you have to be re-born? Interesting. I always figured that for someone to be born again that person had to have a personal experience with Christ. You know, like burning bushes or Paul being thrown to the ground on the road to Damascus

Meanwhile, my new "give it to the angels" policy began to show progress. I received a contract from Big Dog Publishing for *Ralph and Cleo's Krazy Christmas*. The president of Scriptwriter's called and asked if

I would head up a fundraising project for young writers. My angel cards keep telling me, *Go for it, you're safe. Involve yourself with children.* Okay, I thought, here we go. I signed the contract and told Scriptwriter's I'd do it. A producer called and he wanted to do an old play of mine at the Printing Museum Gala. Heracio left a message that he wanted my play *What?* done at his next reading program. Not being a gifted human, my mind can't hold two thoughts at the same time, so with all this activity happening in my life my grief moved back a bit. An angel thought: *Temper your activities with good judgment.* Thank you, God.

Later that week my mouth again broke out in canker sores so badly I could hardly talk. Dr. Cleaver said it was stress and depression and gave me some vile junk to put on them. Personally, I thought it was some sort of 'Job" thing but they soon healed and I went about my business.

My thoughts returned frequently to the last Compassionate Friends meeting. It was a time of anguish but also a time of realizing I wasn't the only person suffering through this. There was a sort of quiet relief. There must be so many people out there somewhere experiencing a devastating loss and feeling like they're the only ones in the world that are feeling this overpowering grief. I vowed to attend every meeting. I felt I had to be there for the mother who walked in like a zombie and the father who was openly crying and totally destroyed. What else could I do? Then an Angel thought: *It's time for a book.* Whoa, now, wait a minute. I'm not an author. I read books, I don't write them. I'm just a story teller, and I tell them through people on a stage.

That night while watching TV in bed I saw an angel standing by the TV. She was small, glowing, smiling, and carrying a book. It happened very quickly and she faded fast, but her luminous wings lingered on for a moment or two. I felt no fear. Maybe it was just the glow of the TV reflected in a darkened doorway. Maybe not.

Sixteen: Fighting Through

It seemed as though my mailbox was stuffed daily with rejections, but it was okay. I was submitting again and that was enough for now. I also received *Questions from Earth – Answers from Heaven*, by Char Margolis. It was an interesting read and I felt I was on a path to somewhere, but for now there were a lot of things I had to do. With Debbie's passing, I not only lost my daughter, but my only child; therefore, my heir. That meant I had to change my will and beneficiary and find an executor for my estate in case I got run over by a bus. Who could it be? It was a matter of trust. Then there was the question of who could this estate be left to. A weighty question. A few days, later a good friend, Paul Young, who had directed some of my plays, called and asked if I was ready to go back to work. We'd been tossing around a work on Nixon. Paul had directed and starred in *Capote Tonight* and he was ready for another challenge. So was I. I ordered up some research books and started digging into Richard M. Nixon, Pat Nixon, his secretary, Rose Mary Woods, and Martha "the mouth" Mitchell. I knew immediately I had picked the right characters for our new venture.

Paul, his wife Katherine, and I had become close friends since *Capote Tonight* and he called often to check on me and Mom. One day while I was thinking about my choice of executor, an angel thought popped into my head: *Paul Young*. I asked him if he would consider doing this for me and he gladly accepted. Then he dropped the bomb. Katherine was seriously ill with ovarian cancer and had had surgery just after Christmas. I was more than a little crazy over the holidays and they were afraid telling me would add to my grief. They were worried about *my* grief when Katherine was in chemo and radiation therapy, both of them not knowing what would happen from day to day. This new Nixon project would be a Godsend for both of us. We could both lose ourselves in it.

Is there really good in everything? Well, I was in big trouble trying to figure out what good could ever come from Debbie's passing or Katherine's illness. And what in the hell was I going to do with this money? I had no close relatives except for Mom, and when she was gone, look out world, it was just me. Maybe something to do with children, since my angel cards were always suggesting my working with children in some way. I put a lot of prayer and meditation into all this and finally asked God to show me a path, because I sure was willing to walk down it to find some answers.

A few days later I was on the net when something familiar popped up. I had once belonged to a service and social sorority, Epsilon Sigma

Alpha, and there it was on my screen. Maybe I could find a Houston chapter and contribute some time to a charity project, find some new friends. I went back to the net and into the ESA site and read that, as their nationwide charity project, ESA had contributed over one hundred million dollars to St. Jude—St. Jude Children's Hospital and Research Center, where parents of a terminally ill child could take their kid to be treated at no cost. I knew that Marlo Thomas had been very involved with St. Jude Children's Hospital since her father, Danny Thomas, founded it. Suddenly, I knew what to do with Debbie's estate. Somewhere, sometime, there would be a mother whose child was desperately ill and had no means to get the help she needed. I read everything I could on St. Jude. I called and talked to them, and the more I learned the more convinced I was that this was what Debbie would have wanted, to help children. She'd spent her whole adult life helping children; why not now? I made an appointment with my attorney and financial advisor and we completed the paperwork. Something good *had* actually happened.

Mother was beginning to fail. She began having accidents in her pants, forgetting that she had eaten, not speaking in whole sentences: dropping a notch mentally and physically every month. It was getting harder for me to take her to activities, especially at night. So I settled for daytime trips and considered myself lucky. I knew I was preparing myself for living without her. I called the funeral director and went over the arrangements. When the time came, all her things would go to the Unity resale shop, Helping Hearts.

***

I was emptying out the garage of the boxes filled with things from Debbie's house and my replacements and donating them to this resale shop. I was still finding things that shattered me: a bottle of her perfume, a broken earring, a box of smell-well packets for the car and closets. I still couldn't let go of her jewelry or the boxes filled with her china and stemware.

One day when I was delivering some of her things to the resale shop, tears running down my face, a volunteer came up, hugged me and said, "I want to tell you something. In 1983, I was on the operating table and I died. Suddenly, my deceased family were all there; my son, my mother, aunt—just everyone. They looked wonderful, young and happy. I can tell you honestly that you'll see your daughter again." I asked the obvious question. "I was sent back," she concluded. By that time she and I, plus two other ladies, were standing in the church parking lot, in the sun, crying. That day my angel cards told me to get rid of clutter. I am, I am, I thought, give me a break here.

I finished the Scriptwriter's project, planted a rose bush, and polished off Char's book on angels. My thoughts drifted back to my family. My dad had passed in my home of liver cancer. I had to bring my folks out of the northeast winter. He was treated at M. D. Anderson Hospital, here in Houston. I didn't remember much except that I was giving him shots of morphine as he was treated at home by our family doctor until the end. I remember him saying to my mother, "My only regret is leaving you." Well, they'd be together soon.

I also wondered if Debbie knew she was going to die and did I also know it in my heart. One day when Debbie first went to the hospital I was in her room looking for a book she wanted me to bring to her. In the bottom drawer of her nightstand, in a blue velvet bag, I found sex toys. At first it took me back and then I kind of smiled and put them away again. After she passed and I was going through everything, they were gone. She'd somehow gotten rid of them when she was home, as if she would have been embarrassed if I had later found them.

I remembered her sitting in one of the recliners at home and she looked like a Buddha. She was a terrible size by then and I thought to myself, she doesn't look good. I begged her to just get her weight down out of the danger zone. Sometimes, when she was home, I'd go to bed early to read while she watched a dog-training or redecorating show and I'd think, I should be out there with her. She'd only be home for the weekend. I could watch the crap shows with her for one night. I had a fear in the pit of my stomach. Did I know? On some level, maybe.

I'd started to collect and read Nixon literature for research. Paul wouldn't let me grieve forever and we had a meeting scheduled for the next week. I started my last Nixon book on the day of our lunch meeting. I'd been right—he wanted to get started.

I checked on Debbie's insurance payments the next day and they were being processed. Ideas and instructions were coming to me daily in meditation. *Write, submit, get rid of clutter*—four more boxes went to church—*read, study*—reading just a few pages was a thing of the past—*plant a memory garden for Debbie and get rid of the dog house.*

Then on March 5th I received a letter from Texas University Medical Branch, Dallas. Debbie was being cremated that day and did I want her ashes sent to me or interned in the hospital's garden. Please send them to me, I replied to their letter. I was going to split them and sprinkle my half on her garden and send her dad the other half. She loved upstate New York, where she was raised, and when she went to visit her dad I knew she felt she was going home.

It had been warm so I set out some grass and prepared pots for her garden. Lots of flowers were to be planted, but after Easter because there could still be one more freeze. Texas, the state of extremes; either the pipes were freezing and breaking or it was ninety-eight degrees for months. We suffered through droughts so bad our yards turned copper—either that, or neighborhoods and underpasses were flooding. I think the next Texas hurricane should be called "Enough Already." But, small blessing, whatever comes down from the sky, you don't have to shovel it.

One Tuesday, UT called. Debbie's ashes would be delivered next week.

Seventeen: Keeping On Track

Life was moving along. I visited my financial advisor and he made an appointment for me with a close friend of his, an attorney, to make the will changes. While in his office, he mentioned he was reading a book called *Heaven* by Randy Alcorn, and recommended it.

I soon learned that my new attorney came to me for a reason. His teenage daughter had been killed a few years prior in an auto accident. He, his wife, and son were devastated. His son, in his grief, began to draw away from the family and the following year his wife, not being able to cope with the loss of their daughter, committed suicide. I understood this. When I learned from the doctors that Debbie had died, my first thought had been *I must go with her so she won't be alone.* I didn't tell him that. His son had gone on to graduate from college and now had an insurance agency. They are very close and have a wonderful working relationship. Of course, I cried my way through this meeting, but I knew he understood why.

***

It was soon the second Tuesday of the month and I attended another intense Compassionate Friends meeting. The church where the meetings were held was a large, sprawling structure that took up the whole block. The building was cream-colored and had lacy green ivy snaking its way up the outer walls. Making my way past ordered gardens to one of the back buildings, I climbed the stairs to the second floor where I found my fellow desolates. The building smelled like an old high school where teenagers had just bounded down the halls from a gym class or a football rally.

The meeting soon turned metaphysical. Strange things were happening to these parents and some, like spirited giraffes, were willing to stick their necks out and talk about them: a very mean cat that suddenly, after the death of his teenage master, became quite loving and for the first time slept on his bed; a mother heard hoop games on her driveway at night. Dreams—a lot of visitation dreams. They were so grateful to God for a visit with their sons or daughters but the general consensus was how horrible it is to wake up and realize that it was just a dream. As reality sets in, they only want to stay, comforted, in the dream.

A psychiatrist spoke about a man running a stop sign one night, killing his seven year old daughter who was in the back seat. In his dreams he talks to God and God to him. His daughter appears and crawls up on his lap and they share stories. She told him that all children who pass go to this giant playground where they are well-attended. They play and have a great time until a parent passes and comes to get them. He cries while telling us this story—and we cry while listening.

Across the table from me was a woman with a book in front of her. It was *Heaven* and she had poems, pictures and all sorts of notes sticking out of it. I felt my angels were kicking me real hard—I went out the next day and bought the book. I've read it twice and bought it for a friend of mine.

In the following days, I had some plays accepted for readings and won a couple of contests. These offerings go in the mail and I don't give them a second thought. They're in God's and my angel's hands and I know that I am loved, safe, and protected in all things. I give a lot of things away to my angels, some small, some large.

Last holiday season Debbie was appalled that I was still using a Polaroid camera. "I didn't think they still made film for those relics," she commented, and surprised me with a digital for Christmas. After schooling me on the camera and the computer program for it, we were happily snapping away. I loved it but after she passed I put it away— I had more on my mind than a camera with memories. Now I was ready to take pictures at some of these play readings and shows, but the camera wouldn't work. Probably the battery, I thought, and tried several times to recharge it. No good. I replaced the battery. No good. I took it to a camera shop; they didn't handle the brand. So I called the manufacturer and their rep told me it was a defective model that had been recalled and they would be glad to replace it.

"When did you buy it?" He asked.

"It was a Christmas gift from my daughter, last year."

I thought the line went dead. Then, "I'm really sorry," he said, but the warranty has run out. I'll be glad to sell you a new one at a discount."

I explained to him, through tears, the story of the camera and how it had been sitting idle through my months of grief. If it had been used, I'd have found out about the recharging problem sooner.

"I'll check with my supervisor and call you back tomorrow," he promised.

No call. At that point I figured I had enough to cry about besides a camera so I just plain gave up the whole problem. "Angels," I said, "Take this camera thing, because I can't handle any more right now." The next day the general manager called to say they were sending me a new camera and paying for the return postage of the old one as well.

***

Debbie's ashes came home. I was at the store when the mailman brought them. He had left a note and I had to chase him down in the neighborhood for my delivery. I felt by his demeanor that he knew exactly what was inside that box. The ashes were felt wrapped in a beautiful copper box but for the life of me I couldn't get the damned thing open. I got a knife and a screwdriver, and, after much prying, jabbing, and swearing—no luck. I had a sudden vision of forcing the thing open and Debbie's ashes flying all over the kitchen and ending up in the dust buster. I could just hear her laughing and saying, "Ohhhhh, Mom." I repacked it, took it to UPS, and sent the whole thing to her father.

***

March was drawing to an end. The taxes were done and the will changed. The new camera came and was working well. As Debbie had two insurance companies involved with her employee insurance, I was still waiting on an additional life insurance check, but things seemed to be calming down some. Paul Young called about the new play and if you can imagine I had my first good laugh on the phone with him telling him about not being able to get the box holding Debbie's ashes open. I even told this story at Compassionate Friends and it was good to laugh and to hear the laughter all around me. Angel message: *There should be a book.*

Easter Sunday, I took Mom to Pam's for dinner and we even talked about Debbie a little. It was a good day, although Pam seemed very down. She really felt the loss of Debbie. They had been great friends and Debbie would often drive over for an over-night visit and they would watch old movies and drink margaritas. I was going to get Debbie and Pam a margarita machine for Christmas, so much for that idea.

That night I had a dream where I was a real estate agent showing a great house but I couldn't see the people who were with me. It didn't matter, because I knew I was going to buy this wonderful house myself and move into it with a man. Who knows who that could have been. I woke up and moved around in the bed. Suddenly, there were my colors floating above me. There were a lot of blue and green patterns blending, separating, and floating on only to return. Then I saw a spark. And it was moving toward me through the colors. It was an eye. I remembered something from my books regarding a third eye. Was this it? Slowly it became two dark brown almond-shaped eyes. Then the forehead was visible. Not the face, only the eyes and forehead, but there was no doubt it was Debbie. I couldn't get enough. I tried to look deeper but was held back. It began to fade and I got up, saying a "Thank You, God." I quickly let the dogs out and made myself a cup of coffee. From then on an eye was part of my meditation, appearing through the colors, and I knew someone was looking out for me. The next day the last of Debbie's insurance money arrived.

Eighteen: Things Are Looking Up

Neglected chores were now a priority. I cleaned the house and porch, had the carpeting cleaned and stretched, deposited the insurance money until I decided what to do with it, and got Mom's and my passport photos. She wasn't going on any long trips, that's for sure, but I had to take her with me and I just couldn't get a passport for myself and not for her.

I had other small repairs done around the house and then had a setback with the director of *Pages*, my short play was selected for the Houston Museum Short Play Competition. Her son was coming home from Iraq and she wanted to go to New York and meet him. We both agreed that was more important than a play. Scriptwriter members stepped in and the play was cast and soon on the right track.

I was doing all these things, but my life seemed mechanical. It was hard to find the joy and I had to look for it, finding blessings every day. My prayers were expanding. Not so much about me anymore but a daily counting of my blessings and asking God to watch over family, friends, and my poor beat up country. My mantra was I am loved, safe, and protected.

I felt the time had come to stop reading about angels and do something constructive. I really wanted to contact my guardian angel. A small, inner voice kept reminding me about having a book to write and I knew I'd need to call on all my angels for their help.

It was spring—it was beautiful. My garden was blooming and fragrant. Jasmine, honeysuckle, and gardenia filled the yard with their heavy aromas. I liked it being light later in the evening. We ate on the porch most days.

During church my pastor talked about body and soul being separate and that I am in control of both. I know I'm not in control of either, and I throw control away to habit and instant gratification. Funny thing about angels: they can't do a darn thing unless asked. So I asked. I asked God to wrap me in angel wings and help me through my grief, as well as giving me patience and understanding while taking care of Mom.

Katherine, Paul's wife, was in the hospital. She'd had her hysterectomy and was now in all kinds of therapy. I told Paul, "As good a playwright as I am, I'm even better at toilet cleaning and cooking." He was doing it all. Katherine called him "my prince" and that he was. He told me once that he had been adopted by a family that already had a son. He dearly loved these people and was well treated. His adopted mother passed away when he was young and, in later life, when Paul was already teaching, his father fell ill with diabetes and had a leg amputated. Paul moved his adopted father in and cared for him until he passed. Not the blood son, but Paul, the adopted son.

I called Unity and had both Mom and Katherine put on their prayer vigil and sent Katherine flowers to cheer her up.

Depression was still my companion. The least little thing threw me into wild sobbing and a sense of loss. Debbie's passing was change happening and I didn't like it one bit, but I knew my angels were hard at work on me. I learned to count my blessings every day, especially those not seen. A sort of "Thank you, God" for my health and Mom's, healing my grief, my abilities, Katherine's healing, prosperity, joy, lifting of depression, my home, family, and even the dogs. I was praying for the ability to do good things with my prosperity while I'm still on planet earth. I was reaching, and it made me feel better because I knew that prayer and meditation were the roads up and out.

The Compassionate Friends meeting that month was held at a park, where they set off balloons in honor of their departed children. Man, I stayed away from things like that. I had enough memories and mementoes that could send me into a fit of anguish without going to an activity that I knew would wipe me out. I read *Ninety Minutes in Heaven* by Don Piper, and tried to understand that good can come from tragedy.

By then I was having no trouble with belief in an afterlife. It was because I wanted to believe it so badly— and so much had happened to support this breakthrough in my spiritual growth. I was still watching John Edward when I could catch his show, and had read another of his books, *One Last Time*. My angel cards were telling me to detox my body, get rid of sugar, and continue on the road to developing a book. During a meditation the cover of the book came to me: a beautiful angel walking in a meadow. There are footprints behind her. Following is a black cocker spaniel looking back around his shoulder at the shadow of a young woman as if to say, "Hurry up, I'm waiting for you."

Debbie had a black cocker spaniel, her name was Silky. She never had another dog after Silky passed away. I found many pictures of her at Debbie's house. I knew this was the cover for my book and that all our pets go to heaven. I also knew that the book would be about dealing with loss, grief, hope, and angels. I was led to Compassionate Friends as comfort but also as a research source, just as I'd be led on many other roads.

I asked God and my angels if I could meet my guardian angel. That night I had a dream of a group of older men dressed in 1920 style clothes. One of them was my grandfather. Could he be my guardian angel? Nice thought.

Sunday, after church, Mom and I had lunch with the youth group. I visited with a woman whose husband had Alzheimer's. She'd put him in a nursing home where he was doing fine, but she was going broke. That concerned me, as my annuities were beginning to suffer in the economic downturn.

Lots of activity going on with the play: directors, actors, Scriptwriters, et cetera. The phone was ringing off the hook with complaints. I kept my mouth shut for a change and tried to move them in a direction of peaceful collaboration. I figured if I stayed calm and didn't add to the conflicts by putting in my two cents of negativity, both me and the situation will benefit. I was learning.

I told Pam the other day on the phone that I would drive to Tomball and pick up both her and her daughter Jennie, and take them to see the plays. After the performance they could stay with me for the night, go to church with us Sunday morning, and then I'd take them to lunch before heading back to Tomball. She was excited, but it didn't happen. What did happen was the producer—or Scriptwriter's president—decided after all the winning plays had been accepted by the museum board that there could be no profanity or, in his opinion, objectionable lines, so he was re-writing all the plays. My new director called me with this information. She also told me that only four playwrights at a time would be seated in the back of the theater, and for only one performance. Then the other four could attend the following night's performance.

I thought my head would explode, but I took it to prayer. Fighting for calm, I called her back and said I would purchase tickets for myself and Mother for whatever performances I decided to attend and sit where I wanted to, since it was open seating. As far as censorship and rewriting my play was concerned, I said, "If he or anyone changes one word of my play, and I'd know, as I'd be at all the rehearsals, I'd pull the play from the production. Further, as an active member of the Dramatists Guild of America, I'd report his actions to the Guild in a New York minute." I said this calmly but firmly and then I hung up and let the whole thing go. Play, director, actors, the whole nine yards. "You got to take this one, God, and send in some angels, because I'm hopping mad and can't handle it right now."

The plays were not changed and went on as written and it was decided all the playwrights could sit where they wanted when they wanted.

When I came out of the theater on opening night I ran into an old writing friend of mine in the lobby. "Where you offended by the profanity?" I asked.

"What profanity?" he answered.

Thank you, God, and my angels, who were working overtime.

I started having trouble with my back. I'd had back surgery two years earlier and my spine was filled with nuts and bolts to keep me together. There was lots of discomfort getting up and down. I had a long prayer and meditation session that morning in bed. It was quiet and dark and the dogs were still beside me and I prayed to God and to my Archangel Raphael that this pain would go away so I could continue with what I had to do: taking care of Mom, the dogs, the house, financial matters, the Nixon play for Paul, and some kind of damned book. The pain vanished and that was that. Thank you, God and my angels.

During the next day's meditation the clouds broke and I saw lots of dog heads floating by. Suddenly, I realized that one looked like Casey. I called for a vet appointment, but before I could get there I noticed he was having a lot of trouble getting up. I saw he had a small lump on his left back leg, and he took a dump in the back room, which he had never done before. The vet found a tumor on his leg. I was scared to death of another loss and turned this whole thing over to God and his mercy. The tumor was removed the following day; malignant, but gone. The vet said a fifty-fifty chance of recurrence. Casey came home and recovered fast. Thank you, God and my angels. There has not been a recurrence.

I was really spooked now. What was going on with this stuff?

When I got really tired of being the caregiver at my house, man, I stopped what I was doing and immediately counted my blessings.

Maybe I'd begun to realize that's what my life's role might be for now: that of caregiver.

I'd been reading my brains out and working on the Nixon play for Paul. *Nixon's Women* was booked into the Houston Fringe Festival that summer. In meditation a small voice, pestered me, "*Get to the book.*" Okay, okay, but I need to finish Nixon first. Katherine was slowly recovering from her surgery but Paul needed an interest, a passion, as badly as I did right then.

What's so amazing about all this is that I'm a control freak. I ran everything and everybody all my life right into the ground. First, I decided that, at age eighty, Mother should move from Florida and move in with me. It was getting hard for her to handle her money and the house. Then I was able to run her and Debbie's life at close range. In time, I transferred all her CD's into an annuity account and set up safeguards for her and Debbie in case something happened to me. Then I decided that when Mom passed, Debbie and I would travel. I would decide who died and who didn't—and when. Then my real father passed away in Florida and I didn't even go to the funeral. Not my life; I had enough trouble. But when Debbie passed and messed up my structured plans, God really got my attention. *Your will, Father, not mine be done.* What's that all about? But since I'd been turning things over to God and my angels to run every day, things were looking up.

Nineteen: You Gotta Keep Truckin'

The rehearsals for the museum play, *Pages*, were a little tattered but it all worked out. It always did. Meditation still revealed lots of colors swirling around and still more vibrant colors flashing inside those clouds. The rotating clouds now contained angel outlines, complete with wings. Sometimes they were even white. They'd stick around for a few seconds and then spiral out of my vision. It was very calming.

Then came the Heparin thing. Fox News reported there had been eighty-one deaths, mostly in the US, due to large doses of Heparin, a drug for thinning the blood to avoid clotting. The deaths were due to an allergic reaction to the drug, as well as from contaminated Heparin from China. The thought that no allergy test was given to Debbie before she was pumped with Heparin that fateful Monday made me crazy. It was in her records; she had been twice to emergency rooms in Houston for hives and once to her doctor in Waco. Was she injected with bad Heparin or given the drug and the hospital not realizing she was having allergy attacks? How could this have happened? I was beside myself with the possibilities. I called my lawyer and then turned it all over to God. How could I face all that again? But somehow it felt right. I must find the courage to at least look into this. Finally, I forwarded all the e-mail information on Heparin to my lawyer and pushed it from my mind, trying to go about my business. Months later I received the medical reports from my lawyer. Debbie had passed while in good hands, medically and spiritually.

Then more trouble at rehearsal. Janice, an actress, had a car problem and couldn't make it; Sammy had an emergency at the airport; Alex had a home break-in. Nobody showed up for rehearsal. I was really down now. Is life only to deal with loss and disappointment? Now, that was a crap thought! Angel cards: keep cool, keep joyous, keep compassionate, keep loving, and then my own thought: keep quiet.

I was really into reading *Heaven* and taking it real slow. There were a lot of new concepts for me to digest. Lots of questions. Where is Debbie? What's she doing? Am I going to be there, too? Am I just going to float around or will I be busy doing things? What's this angel thing?

I started to work on *Nixon's Women* for Paul.

***

Pages opened and it was great. I invited Paul and Katherine to the opening and, as usual, they were charming. It was Katherine's first outing. I never saw anyone who could part a theater crowd like Paul. He's like the Pied Piper of theater. We were really pleased with the play and audience reaction. Attending the cheese and wine reception after the performance, I realized that taking care of Mom's needs pulled me away from what I should have been doing at this function: meeting actors, directors, and whoever was there who could have put a script to work. I spent most of the time seeing that her cup and plate were filled and that she was feeling all right. The realization was something I needed to think about.

***

I read a few more chapters of *Heaven* and watched a few more of John Edward's shows as he channeled spirits. Is this for real? I'd done enough reading, grieving, and being tired. I had to know what this was that I was going through. I wanted to talk to a psychic, but didn't know where to find a good one, where to even start. Well, stupid, I thought, you belong to a metaphysical church. What better place? I'd already checked phonebooks, newspapers, the net, and come up with lots of possibilities, but nothing that felt right. That next Sunday I was in the Unity bookstore browsing and there it was: "Tranquility," a holistic newsletter. I grabbed it and found weird things being offered; I didn't have a clue as to what they were. What in the hell were Indigo kids, Reiki Healing, and Ion Foot Baths? Then I saw "Grief Therapy within a Channeling Circle." That sounded like what I'd been looking for. It was an evening session, so I got a sitter and found Tranquility Center. It was just down the street from Dr. Cleaver's office and I drove right to it. Surprise. It's an older home in a suburban setting that has been remodeled to accommodate the holistic world. Lots of work rooms, lots of windows and light, lots of activity, a sparkling kitchen with snacks set out, and always hot coffee on the burner. From what I could see it was surrounded by informal gardens; tables, chairs, and benches were strewed about so you could sit and talk, and they provided ample parking all around the place.

I signed in and entered one of the large work rooms. At one end there was a smiling, attractive blonde woman, a psychic, just finishing up a tarot card reading. I was expecting gypsy costumes, woven rugs, and hanging beads and what I got was Jasmine Jones, dressed in everyday street clothes, with a high-low haircut, eating a cookie.

There were about fifteen of us in the room. Jasmine came over and joined our group as she popped the rest of her cookie into her mouth. She was our leader and introduced herself. Jasmine went around the room giving readings and it seemed to me that most of the people in the room knew her quite well. They laughed and talked back and forth with her, asking questions and with them responding to her answers. She would stop occasionally while talking with someone and sort of tilt her head to the side, getting very quiet, as if she was listening to someone, and then continue with the reading. Soon it was my turn. She looked at me, did her quiet thing and said, "What is it you'd like to know?"

"I want to know about my angels and spirit guides."

After a moment, "Well, you have lots of angels around you, but five stay pretty close, as you keep them busy. You've always kept them busy. You also have a male spirit guide who is very intellectual, and who sometimes wears animal skins. He has been helping you for a long time." Hot damn, maybe we were going to get somewhere.

"In meditation I see an eye all the time now. What's that all about?"

"I also see the eye. It could be your third eye. Investigate this. Your angels are surrounding you—lots of color. You are extremely protected. Have you had a loss?

"Yes, my daughter."

I knew I was saying too much, but I was drawn in and I was getting so many hits. Male spirit guide writing through me, the colors floating around me, and five hovering angels? My head was spinning.

"Keep a dream journal. If you can't remember what you dreamed ask your angels to help you remember. Ask your angels for their help. They cannot help you unless you ask. Especially your master guide."

"I'm very concerned about my mother's health and her passing."

"Don't be. Debbie will be in the light for your mom. Is there anything else?

"Not today, thank you." I was wiped out. I had not told her Debbie's name.

***

I went out and bought a tape recorder and transcriber the next day. A book was beginning to materialize. I also started re-reading my angel books.

All of a sudden it was May, seven months and what changes in my life. I continued morning "thank you" prayer and meditation, spiritual readings, angel cards, and construction of a journal going back to when Debbie first got sick in preparation for the book. Slow going on that; I could only do a few days at a time before I was reduced to mush.

I was trying very hard to be open to suggestions and directions from spirit guides and angels while working on Nixon's Women for Paul. He wanted it yesterday. Bless him. Katherine was up and about and she was in my prayers every day. I made an appointment for a "Third Eye" workshop at Tranquility for the next week, planted a rose bush in Debbie's garden, and hung an angel wind chime in the pear tree. Did I still bubble up? Every day. I wished I could just sleep through Mother's Day and I had already planned to keep myself very busy.

Had my life changed? You bet.

Twenty: Angel Reading

It was a busy Sunday. A cool front had blown down from the North and it was a beautiful spring day. There was an afternoon party at Travis', the president of Scriptwriters/Houston, house that afternoon and I was planning to go after my reading. That's right; I had an appointment with a psychic. My appointment was with Tamara, who conducts angel therapy workshops at Tranquility. The center's garden was in full bloom, trees and bushes green and lush from all the rain we'd had lately. There were people of all ages milling about, waiting for readings or other therapies; all happy, all laughing and visiting with each other. There was a foreign-looking man in the back garden setting up musical instruments for an entertainment later in the day. I learned this was Ah-Shan. I was to see him again. I was escorted and introduced to Tamara, who was a motherly blonde, with short hair and green eyes. She greeted me warmly and we got to work.

ANGEL READING WITH TAMARA
AT TRANQUILITY SPIRITUAL CENTER 5/3/08

(HIT indicates a statement made to me that hit home. Tamara could not have known this.)

Pat: Tell me your name again?

Tamara: My name is Tamara.

Pat: Tamara. Okay.

Tamara: And your name is?

Pat: Pat Morgan. Tamara, can I take one of your cards?

Tamara: Sure. First, I like to tell people that what I'm picking up on is in this moment of time. Because God gave you free will, you can either speed it up, slow it down, or change it all together. If you don't have real drama in your life, you can change that as well. You have the will power to do that. You can make any changes you want in the way you live your life. So is there anything in particular that you're looking to know?

Pat: Yeah. I'd like to know who my guardian angel is. Jasmine was channeling for me yesterday and said I had a lot of angels around me—four or five—and they are all protecting me and I've kept them all very busy all my life.

Tamara: Yes.

Pat: And, uh, let's see ... what else did she say? I'd like to know about those angels and the fact that when I meditate I see lots of colors.

Tamara: Okay.

Pat: Lots of swirling colors and in the middle of those colors is like bright flashes of light: indigo, cobalt. Sometimes I get a quick image, sometimes I don't.

Tamara: Those colors belong to the Archangel Michael.

Pat: Amber is very prominent. The amber goes in and out and swirls about almost constantly in and out of the other colors.

Tamara: Is it more of a gold color than an amber?

Pat: Well, at first I thought it was gold and then well, thinking about it maybe, it's not gold, maybe it's more amber.

Tamara: Usually when the gold color comes through it indicates the Christ consciousness. The ascended Master of Christ has come in. And that's not uncommon to have that color coming in with Michael.

Pat: I have blue, sometimes a different blue, a dark blue and then a medium blue, and then the amber, sometimes I have a purple, sometimes I'll get an eye.

Tamara: Hmmm.

Pat: One time I got two eyes. I mean the one eye expanded into two eyes. They were dark brown and almond shaped. There was not a doubt in my mind that those eyes were the eyes of my daughter.

Tamara: Uh-huh.

Pat: Oh, a couple weeks ago I got images of dogs. They weren't dogs that I recognized except all of a sudden I thought, *Wow*, that one looks like Casey. So I called the vet because it was time for him to have an annual checkup anyway and he found a tumor on his leg. It was removed two days later. So something was going on. Something's always going on with this. That is why I'm trying to be very open to what's happening in meditation. What I'm getting and what's going on in my life and what opportunities are opening up. And I'm trying to follow through with the thoughts that are coming to me because I know that they're not me; it sounds like me, but then I don't know. Maybe angels?

Tamara: You know you're a very clairvoyant person. Clairvoyant means "clear see." You're seeing from your third eye. That's the way you're receiving your information, which is typically the most common way for a lot of people to receive their information. The next thing for women is the clairsentience or "clear feeling." You feel things— vibrations. You feel energies around you, things like that. Ahh, probably Debbie (HIT) was coming through telling you about the dog.

Pat: Debbie, she—

Tamara: I know. Okay. Uh, do you often feel someone touch you on your shoulder?

Pat: No, I'm not aware of it, if it happens.

Tamara: She's showing me by doing this on my shoulder. She comes in and she kind of does like this. (Hand slightly above her shoulder) That's what she does.

Pat: I know she's around me.

Tamara: Yes. She's definitely around you and she's always doing this. She's always kind of like doing this thing with the shoulder.

Pat: But she's fully passed over and she's fine?

Tamara: Yes. She's fine. She's totally fine. In fact, they're telling me about her thing over there and she's not going to be coming back here for a very, very long time. Her thing over there is that she's going to be working with small children. They're showing me a lot of small children. She's used to working with children. (HIT)

Pat: Debbie worked with children.

Tamara: Yes. She's going to be working with a lot of small children. And she keeps telling me, "Mother, I'm fine, Mother, I'm fine, Mother, I'm fine. (Chuckle) So I'm getting this picture of her slim. I'm not sure if this is the way she wants to look or if it's the way she really looks. Because she's showing me that she's slender. (HIT) She's got hair about down to here. It's kind of a — what do you call it, I don't know what color you'd call that? It's kind of dark and straight. (HIT)

Pat: She was dark haired.

Tamara: Yeah, it's dark. Not black, but dark.

Pat: She was dark haired and she was morbidly obese.

Tamara: Well, she's slender on the other side. I can tell you that.

Pat: She wouldn't take that with her?

Tamara: No. Illness and all infirmities stay here. She's very slender and she's wearing white. I'll call it a dress but it's a very Roman looking outfit. That's what she's wearing but she's saying, "Mother, I'm fine. And she's been assigned to take care of the children. That's her deal over there. Ah, she's telling me that she's going to send you flowers. (BIG HIT)

Pat: Debbie always sent me flowers on Mother's Day.

Tamara: Well, she's sending flowers. So somehow or some way you're going to get flowers. I don't know if they'll arrive on Mother's Day, but she's going to send you flowers because she's showing me a yard and she's showing me flowers.

Pat: Well, I made a memorial garden for her out in the backyard.

Tamara: But she's showing me flowers. She's going to send you flowers. Have they not bloomed yet? Have some of the flowers in the garden not bloomed?

Pat: Some of them are blooming, some aren't.

Tamara: Well, she's going to send you flowers. So be aware of that yard. Be watching for it, because there's something that's going to draw your attention. And it's going to be her sending these specific flowers. They look something like roses but it's not a rose. It's got real pretty petals and such but it's not a rose because she's not showing me it's got thorns, but it's really pretty. I don't know what it is but it's very pretty and—

Pat: What color is it?

Tamara: It's kind of what I would call almost a reddish/pink color. Not really pink and not really red, kind of a reddish/pink color. But more red. Yes, red.

Pat: I don't know, but I'll watch what blooms.

Tamara: It's like that, but she's showing me distinctly that she's going to send you flowers.

Pat: Okay.

Tamara: So kind of watch it. And did you know that the 10th is Mother's Day in Mexico?

Pat: No, I didn't know that.

Tamara: Yep. Saturday is Mother's Day in Mexico and Sunday is Mother's Day here. It doesn't always happen that way, but technically that's the way it is this year. So be kind of aware that we've got two Mother's Days coming up right together. So be on the lookout, because she's sending you flowers.

Pat: Tell me about all these angels that are floating around.

Tamara: Well, the thing about angels is they come and go as you need them.

Pat: Okay.

Tamara: So you can have hundreds of angels at one time. They each have a different function, different purpose, whatever you're working on at the time. Actually, you've got an archangel working with you right now and his sole purpose is to help your grieving. He's helping you through this. So be aware that he's around. He's giving you comforting. And he kind of gets a bad rap because he's known as the Angel of Death.

Pat: I know him. I've read his card. Who is he?

Tamara: Azreal. I know him very well because he does a lot of readings with me. And he's there to help you through it. Okay. He's already helped your daughter cross over so that's no big deal. But, he's here to help you through it and you'll get through it. Okay, the most important thing for you to remember is that she's here – she'll always be here. Now, the thing about a departed one is when they cross over, they still retain a bit of their personality.

Pat: Okay.

Tamara: And they don't always come when you call them. They have that choice. I'll give you an example of my father. He has an assignment over there and sometimes when I really need him and I call for him he can't come because he's busy doing other stuff. So I get a "gone fishing" sign. It flashes: gone fishing, gone fishing. And he's sending me that flashing sign to let me know "I'm busy, call back later." That's what I get, so I say, okay. Then I know not to continue trying to contact him for a while. It's something similar with your daughter. When she's not available to come because she's working with the children, she's going to send you some kind of sign that will let you know: I'm okay, but I can't come right now. Okay, she's showing me a bell. You're going to hear a bell. That's what she's showing me, a little bell. So if you're calling Debbie and you hear a bell, forget it because she's not coming. So understand that when you hear a bell she can't come right then, but any other time she can come and you can have a full fledged conversation with her, because she's sitting right here.

Pat: Is she going to answer me?

Tamara: She'll answer you in a way you can understand. For example, taking into consideration that you're clairvoyant, she may send you a picture, a flash of a picture like a mini-movie or snap shot or a color, or you may see something on the side of the road that will answer your question. For you, it's going to be visual.

Pat: What's this purple? Is that an aura? Maybe it's her aura.

Tamara: Well, when you cross over like she did the aura is always white.

Pat: Oh, I see.

Tamara: It's always white. Because once you cross over you're in a higher state of consciousness than you are on this side.

Pat: She was really into all this. I didn't realize how much until after she passed. Then I had to go through all her things and I found her angel cards, tarot cards, angel kits, books, stuff she would try to read to me, but I didn't take it seriously. I just thought it was something for her to do. But she was into metaphysical things more than I ever realized until after she passed. Once, she was sitting on the bed and I was putting away her laundry and she said, "Mother, it's okay because my angels are around me."

Tamara: Oh, yeah. That's the cool thing about this, because once you understand that angels are there you'll never be alone. It's so much easier to accept the fact that death is not death; it's just a new beginning. Okay. You have a multitude of angels around you coming and going. Azreal, he's the one that works through the grieving with you, and, of course, Michael is working with you because he's there with you all the time.

Pat: I read in one of the books I'm reading that I had four: Michael, Gabriel, Raphael, and Uriel.

Tamara: Yes, but you also have Chamuel working with you. What he's working with you on is relationship and companionship issues. He also helps you find things.

Pat: Good. Help me find my ring. Make it appear. (I'd lost it in the dryer.)

Tamara: But Chamuel is about relationships with you. It's about healing relationships, creating relationships and ... Okay, he's telling me you avoid relationships and fear relationships with other people. There is a trust issue with you. You have a hard time trusting. People are attracted to you. They like your energy. They're comfortable with you and it's almost like people want to attach themselves to you, and what's happening is that you haven't learned to deal with it or control it in the past. You take so much of other people's stuff on yourself that you've gotten confused as to what's yours and what's theirs. And it's a very simple technique. Just be sure Michael's there okay? In order not to absorb other people's stuff and get it confused with your own, which happens to a lot of people, it's simple— every day call in Michael and say, "Michael, cut all cords, known and unknown, to me that block my path." And it will ease you up. When you're in the shower imagine that the water is washing all the debris off of you. Say, "Michael, let this water heal me, let this water take away anything that is not mine and no longer serves me. And let that healing start." And I think as you clear yourself and you don't feel like people are attaching themselves to you you'll learn to trust again.

Pat: I feel like I'm imposed upon.

Tamara: I know, it's like they're physically attaching themselves to you, because you have that energy. You know, you'd be a great healer if you chose to be. But with that comes responsibility. With that comes knowing you're not going to take on other people's stuff, and that's when you push people away, because it's like you say, "I can't take on any more stuff. I'm so full of my own stuff I can't take on any more." It's a problem of not cleaning yourself. When I get up in the morning, instead of calling all this stuff up, I call in my Archangels, Michael, Raphael, Gabriel, Ariel, and Azreal. I call them my big five. And then I say, "Protect my home, protect me, my children, and clear the debris out." And I walk with them all day and I know that they'll shield me. Then I ask them very simply as I visualize them—and you're good at that. I visualize a pipe running all the way through my chakras, yes, running down me into core of the earth and I ask them to take anything that is not mine that does not serve me, and put it into that pipe so it dissipates into either heaven or earth. And I don't take on anybody else's stuff. It's not mine. It's not my responsibility. It's their stuff. I'll help them deal with it but I won't take it.

Pat: Okay

Tamara: And I think that's where you need to go. To get yourself in a state where you don't feel like you're taking on everybody's else's stuff and you're not holding onto it. And I think that once you do that you'll feel more able to be receptive to other people, knowing that, yes, they have issues; yes, they're going to want to attach themselves to you, but you say, "I can give them guidance but I can't fix it." It's not mine to fix but I will give them suggestions and guidance and leave it there. And what you'll find is that those people who are desperate to give their stuff to other people because they don't want to deal with it, those people will just fall away. They will leave your life. Then you'll get the responsible, friendly, supportive, people to come to you. And that's where you're headed. You're still in the grief process. You know, no one knows how long it's going to take anybody to grieve over anything. It's just how quickly you move through it. You know, when my grandfather passed away not long ago, I mean, I knew he was going. We had already finished our stuff, like saying our goodbyes. And when he passed away I was over it. I was glad he was gone because he was out of pain and I knew where he was going and I knew my dad and my grandmother was there waiting for him. So it was knowledge that helped me get over his passing real fast. When my dad died it wasn't that way. It took me over a year to get over him. I had a really good friend explain it to me. You know, like why he had to go, what he was doing, et cetera.

Pat: Well, this is going to take me some time.

Tamara: Yes.

Pat: I have a group support helping me.

Tamara: Good, because in our form we need the human contact.

Pat: I know.

Tamara: It's just part of it. It's part of being human.

Pat: We were very, very close, and she was my only child.

Tamara: But, like I said, I know she's around you almost all the time. She may not be there in human form, but they're always there for us and it's almost like — and I tell everyone who will listen that my dad and I can still really fuss.

Pat: Well, (laughing) Debbie and I could really fuss. We could really get into it pretty good. We are hard-headed, both of us.

Tamara: But you'll notice. Pay attention, because you're going to start noticing things about the most familiar things when she's there. Pay attention, though. Be aware, because when my dad comes in it's usually in the car when I'm driving. Because he taught me to drive, I guess. Anyway, it's usually when I'm driving, and I smell Shiner's beer and menthol cigarettes. I don't even think they make Shiner's beer anymore.

Pat: Every once in a while I get a whiff of something. I'll be sitting in my chair in the living room and it's like flowers or air freshener is behind me. At first I didn't know what it was, and then I thought, I know what it is. Debbie's here.

Tamara: And that's when you should start talking to her, because she's right here. And with you being so visual, like I said, you're going to start seeing things. And don't let it frighten you.

Pat: Yes, Debbie would never do anything that would frighten me.

Tamara: But sometimes they startle us, so pay attention to your vision. Or you might start seeing like the way I see it, it's like shadows. Sometimes behind you, or a quick flash or something. They're doing that because they want to let you know they're there but they're trying not to frighten you. But it does frighten some people that don't understand. But as you progress more and more you're going to see more. You might even see the person. So it's a process. So be aware of that. Don't forget the flowers.

Pat: Well, I got flowers for Mother's Day every year for maybe twenty-five years and I could hardly focus on this year (I'm crying now) and I didn't know how I was going to handle it. It felt like I wanted to get on a plane and go someplace. You know, I just didn't know. And then for you to say that.

Tamara: She keeps showing me this garden and this one flower.

Pat: Well, she has a memorial garden in my backyard, and I just put some new plants in there. Flowers, a new red rose bush that is really blooming now. But there's a pink one, too.

Tamara: It's kind of a pinkish red color.

Pat: I don't know. But some of them haven't bloomed, so we'll see.

Tamara: You're going to notice it because it's going to be different than the surrounding flowers. It's going to be different from anything else.

Pat: Okay. I'll look for it. That's cool.

Tamara: That's what she's showing me. Do you have any questions?

Pat: I don't think so today.

Tamara: Just know you have a lot of angels and they're with you all the time. In fact—

Pat: Is there a male in there? Jasmine mentioned something about there being a male master guide.

Tamara: A master guide?

Pat: Yes. She was telling me about a male master guide that was working with me.

Tamara: Well, I see you working with Christ. Christ is considered the Master guide. Jesus, He's the Master guide. That's why the gold.

Pat: The gold is very predominant in my meditations.

Tamara: Jesus is the Master guide in most circles. I also see you working with a goddess named Lilith.

Pat Lilith?

Tamara: Yeah, I'm seeing you with Lilith. Why are you working with her?

Pat: Is she a spirit guide or is she a goddess?

Tamara: She's a goddess. (She was hunting through the bookshelf.)

Pat: On a different level then?

Tamara: Oh, yes, there's a lot of different levels. Like there's a multitude of levels up there that we don't ever touch, but we have the archangels, we have general angels, then we have the ascended masters, and then we have what we call our spirit guides, and then we have the deceased. Those are the levels. Then there's a lot of other levels beneath these levels. But what we mostly concentrate on are these levels, these major levels.

Pat: Okay

Tamara: Then, like I said, there are a whole lot of different levels up there that you'd see on very complicated charts and things like that. But you're working through archangels, an ascended Master, and goddesses that fall into this category.

Pat: Lilith?

Tamara: But, uh, okay. They're also telling me, wasn't there a Lilith in the Bible? There are a lot of references to Lilith in the Bible. And Lilith got a bad rap in the Bible. But don't get that confused with the Goddess Lilith. There's a lot of information about Lilith. Okay. You're in a transition. And she deals with beauty and transitions.

Pat: Well, I'm too old to be concerned with the beauty end of it, but the transition, that's interesting. What could that be about?

Tamara: I think the beauty is that you can see the beauty in life—but you're not seeing it anymore.

Pat: I don't. It's like the joy has gone out of my life.

Tamara: That's what she's telling you. You need a transition, a transition into your new reality; because you have a long time and you don't want to spend it grieving.

Pat: I sure don't.

Tamara: And the transition is coming to you. She's telling me that, since your daughter is working with children, have you ever thought about it?

Pat: No. Not so much with children but with grief, with grieving. I'm getting, like, to write a book. I'm getting lots of stuff about making a change and doing a book regarding the grieving. I'm getting a put your stuff in order—my plays—and start the book. So I'm getting ready. I even bought myself a recorder and transcriber. My angels have been very insistent I do this. Apparently, this is something I need to have made the investment in order to get going on it.

Tamara: I don't want to stop you, but they're telling me something here. There's grief, from a parent/child point of view? There's a parent leaving a child or a child leaving a parent. I think it would be cool to have a grandfather leaving his daughter without fear, especially for the granddaughter.

Pat: I've been to some Compassionate Friends meetings. The first time, I literally crawled in there. I still don't talk very much because I cry so hard, but I get a real feeling that some went every month to tell the story of the death over and over and over. These same people, over three-four months, I was hearing the same death stories over and over. And I thought, okay, but what are you doing for yourselves to move out of it? I'm not hearing healing; I'm hearing only grief. And I'm not hearing any steps to get better. And that's when the book came to me. I'm going to have to do this, to write about my own grief, to have them recognize that there are steps you can take to relieve this horrible pain. The hole will be there, but there are other things that can be put in this hole to reduce it.

Tamara: Well, it's not so much the hole will be there. The hole will heal. It's about letting the heart open enough to know that's it's just a change, that angels will be there.

Pat: What amazed me about it was I was looking at people with a loss of four-five years. I was maybe two-three months into it and I knew I couldn't feel like this same way four-five years from now. I know I can't.

Tamara: Yes, and it's a choice. I'm going to tell you that it's a choice you make in realizing she's not gone, and there's a lot of stuff she can help you with from the other side. Things she and your angels can help you accomplish. And it's not an ending; it's a new beginning and a change in the relationship. But I understand what you said, because my dad's been gone since '81 and my mother is still mad at him. But it's her choice not to get over it.

Pat: That's right.

Tamara: No matter how much I talk to her and try to help her ...

Pat: It's not a matter of getting over it. I don't think I'll ever get over it but it has to move, this pain. It has to sort of soften.

Tamara: Like I said, it becomes a new relationship, but the memories of the old relationship will still exist. They will never leave you. It will just take a deeper form and that is where you have to move to. That's what's going on. That's your transition. The memories are there. They'll always be there. However, the physical relationship has moved to different level, a different place. And that's where you're going to have to go with this relationship.

Pat: This is going to take time.

Tamara: Yes, it's not an easy time or easy thing.

Pat: There's been so many things since I've made an effort to open up to different experiences, so much has come in.

Tamara: Oh, yeah.

Pat: There's been so much opportunity in things for me to be doing.

I've been winning prizes and winning playwright contests and doing this and doing that and opportunities, like I need you to write this or that for me, things like that. Things are opening up so much and I believe it's because I'm more in tune with what's coming through while I'm sitting quietly and meditating and tuning in to guidance through my angel cards. The messages are clear. Get your priorities straight, get writing because this is something that needs to be done, and what you want to do financially will be taken care of.

Tamara: She's coming in to tell me something. Take it for what it is. Something about her tarot cards. (HIT) But she's telling me for you to feel the energy in those cards and to spread them out on the floor and look at them. Just look at them, the pictures. There's something in those cards that will pop out at you. Every time you spread them across the floor something different is going to pop out. And you're going to understand it. There's a message in those cards for you. Don't pay any attention to reading tarot, but just pay attention to the pictures.

Pat: Okay.

Tamara: And understand that some of the pictures, for example, when you see the Hanged man, all the Hanged man means is transition. For example, when you see the card of death it doesn't mean literally death, it means change.

Pat: She has all this stuff. I don't know what she was doing with all this but she had it all, even books on palm reading. I mean, she was really getting into this and her cousin, Pam, was into it with her. I said to her cousin one day, "I can't believe Debbie didn't have crystals."

Tamara: She did. (HIT)

Pat: "Oh," Pam answered, "she had crystals."

Tamara: She did. I'm surprised you haven't found them yet.

Pat: Well, I cleaned out everything at her house. Now, I may have found them and tossed them because I didn't know what they were.

Tamara: Yeah. You probably just thought they were rocks. And I see them folded up in something.

Pat: Well, I've been through everything, and unless they were folded up in something and they got tossed, because all this happened very quickly. I had to clean her house out and I had boxes of stuff going to Goodwill, boxes going to her dad in New York, and boxes going home with me. There was food that had to go to the church pantry, and boxes of her things to be sold. It was a nightmare and I did all this in twelve days. So about her crystals, now, they had to be close to her because her angel cards were close and she used to sit on the bed while she was recovering and do her angel cards. So I said to Pam, "Those crystals had to have been close." She told me Debbie's crystals were in a velvet bag. And I said, "Well, I found a velvet bag but there's only jewelry in it." I haven't been through her jewelry yet. I can't do that yet.

Tamara: Yes.

Pat: But I have no idea where they are, but maybe they'll show up someday. She had carry bags in her car with all this physic stuff in it and I would have thought her crystals would have been in one of those carry bags.

Tamara: You know, typically people have their crystals all over. I have mine all over my house. I have them disbursed in a grid, like a formation, all over my house.

Pat: I found one. A heart shaped rose quartz.

Tamara: I do have one little bag that I use, that I carry, just a little bag. But the rest of my crystals are disbursed all over my house.

Pat: As I said to her cousin, wherever they were they were close by her. They may have been in her night stand and got shoved to the back. When I sold the bedroom set they may have gone with it. I don't know where they are. If I had found them, at that time I was in such shock when I was doing all this, and of course, I'm certainly not where I was six months ago, and, as I said I might have found that bag and said, "Oh, now what in the hell's this?"

Tamara: You could have even thought they were marbles.

Pat: Yes, I could have. I sure as hell had lost mine.

Tamara: When my paternal grandmother passed away I thought she was a holy roller. She made all the boys go to church, but she never made me go. I really thought she was big in her church and she probably thought I was a devil or something. I was strange even then. But when I was going through her stuff and cleaning out her drawers there was this big pile of handkerchiefs, the old fashioned kind. And I was putting the handkerchiefs in a box and at the bottom of those handkerchiefs I found a clear quartz stone. It exactly matched the one I had in my pocket. I'd bought it at a place here in Houston, but it exactly matched the one I found. I just couldn't believe that she had that in with all her stuff.

Pat: Well, Debbie had them, and they're somewhere, and I truly believe that they were close by her. Probably by her cards or someplace like that but I wasn't looking for them either. And they weren't tucked into where all the other stuff was. So I assume she had them closer to her because she was using them.

Tamara: A lot of people do this. They even use their jewelry.

Pat: This smoky topaz ring I'm wearing is one of hers. And I have other stones, too. I have jewelry that was hers that I'm going to go through someday.

Tamara: It may be that the crystals are hidden in the jewelry.

Pat: Very well could be, because she had two jewelry boxes and this velvet bag, but I just have not been able to go through that yet. I pulled the bag open because I thought the crystals had to be in there, but it just looks like old pearls and some of her grandmother's things. So I just tied it up and put it away. Someday I'll go through all that but not now.

Tamara: These are all precious stones. (She was showing me her necklace.) For different purposes and for what I learn from them.

Pat: They're beautiful. Are these quartz? What's this one up here? Is that a rose quartz? I found one of those in the shape of a heart, but that came out of a Doreen Virtue Angel Kit. It was in there. She had that kit and she had one where you roll dice.

Tamara: The Guidance Kit?

Pat: Yes. She had that, and all that other stuff. You know, we belonged to Unity Church years ago and I got away from it because it really got a little spooky for me.

Tamara: Which one?

Pat: I was going to the pyramid.

Tamara: I'm sorry, I tried to go there several times, but I know some people who still go there.

Pat: I go to Unity Northwest now.

Tamara: I know where Northwest is, too. But I had a problem going into the pyramid.

Pat: I don't even think the pyramid's there anymore, is it?

Tamara: Yeah, the pyramid's there but they're using it for a lecture hall.

Pat: I knew they bought land while I was there and they were going to build this big church. And when that happened I thought maybe I ought to get back to the church, but I didn't want to drive all the way over to the pyramid. Also it's so big. Then I found this little Unity Church, off Grant Road, and I really like it. And that's where I found your brochure. I'd been going through the phone book, because I said somewhere there's a place where I can get some answers. And there was your brochure sitting right in front of me last Sunday and I thought, well, there's the answer to that. That's the kind of stuff that's been happening. I say, well, I need this, and all of a sudden there it will be.

Tamara: We're in a common manifestation right now, a great time. It's almost like what you think—happens. And you'd better be careful of your thoughts, because you just might get it. That's an old adage, but it's very true right now. What you think, you manifest.

Pat: Let's go back to me working with children. (I was beginning to get it together.) In a roundabout way—yes, this is true. Debbie was a drug and alcohol counselor for kids. And … I worked hard all my life, invested well, so there would be money for Debbie and I wouldn't have to worry about her. (Crying) Well, when she passed, there goes the heir. There is no one else but my mom and she's ninety-two. That's where I thought it was going to hit. I was prepared for that one. Not Debbie. But, when I pass, that money is going to St. Jude's Children's Hospital in Debbie's name. So there are children involved in this somewhere. I decided on St. Jude's because somewhere, whether it's now or later, there are going to be mothers who are going to get these death sentences for their children and they'll have no money and no insurance. The one reason why I chose this place is because St Jude's pays for everything. They pay and it doesn't matter if you have insurance or not, or if you don't have any money, they pay for the whole shot: travel, hospital, whatever. Now, I've said I need five million more. That's what I want. I've put that out there. It costs one million dollars a day to run this hospital. And I said I want five million more, so now other things are coming up for me—the book, for one thing.

And another thing that's happened, have you been aware of this Heparin thing? It's a blood thinner drug they've been getting out of China and eighty-three people have died, most of them in Texas. And, well, Debbie got that staph infection, that Super Bug, and they operated on her twice and they got it and they pretty well felt that she beat it. And she was going back to work the next week and was more than doing good. And then she came home for a few days and said to me on Thursday morning, "I don't feel good." She was gone Monday. It was blood clots that had formed in her legs. Of course, her weight didn't help anything. Anyway, I was told they went to her heart. But the last day she was having so much trouble breathing and I was at the hospital in Temple, Grossman Memorial, and I said to her I was going to take her grandmother home and see to the dogs and then I'll be back and she said she would see me later. I told her I would call her before I left. She said okay and was kind of napping, but when I called, they put the doctor on and he said she couldn't breathe and he was working on her right then and he was rushing her down to ICU to put a trachea in. And she died before they could get it in. She died before I could get there. But this drug that they were pumping into Debbie was the same drug, Heparin, the one I was hearing about, the blood thinner, because of the clotting. And I called my attorney the other day and said could this have possibly been an allergic reaction to this drug because she swelled up and she couldn't breathe.

Tamara: And it's like a shock.

Pat: And that's exactly how this drug killed all these people. So he said to talk to her dad and see what goes. We could go into a lawsuit very easily right now.

Tamara: Is there a class action suit going on?

Pat: I don't know, but I'm going to ask the attorney next week when I call him and ask him if this would be a class action suit or is this just going to be us. He said we have to set up a trust so that any funds we get could go into this fund. I don't understand that. If I sue them why do I have to have a trust? (This proved to be invalid; no trust is needed.)

Tamara: Well, what he's trying to do is protect the taxation area of it.

Pat: Maybe.

Tamara: Because when you win a certain type of law suit—

Pat: It's taxable income.

Tamara: Certain types of trusts are taxable income. And when you start talking in the millions of dollars, well, trusts handle it differently. Because there's a difference between compensatory damages and punitive damages in the way they're taxed. One of them is taxable and one of them is not. It depends on how they structure the settlement for the compensatory or punitive.

Pat: I'll have to ask him about that.

Tamara: And they're taxed differently. I forget which is which, but the one our attorneys got on my dad was not taxable.

Pat: Well, that's the one we need to get. And then if this money goes into this trust, the trust will be left to St Jude's. Well, I don't know, but all these things are opening up and I've asked for five million. It could come from the proceeds from the book, the lawsuit. I don't know, God, I'm just asking for it. And God is going to have to handle it. But I don't know if I can go through it all again. Look at me; I'm a mess.

Tamara: Look at it this way. You're going to have to make a decision. The doctors/hospital's insurance company may want to settle with you on a personal basis or you could let it go into a full-fledged class action suit that could draw out several years. So you have a choice to make. Are you going to settle for interest money or are you going to let it go into a class action suit and possibly let it go on for years.

Pat: I don't know.

Tamara: That's your decision.

Pat: That's a decision based on what they tell us.

Tamara: Exactly.

Pat: And the attorneys, they take at least fifteen percent?

Tamara: Yes, most of the time they take it on a contingency basis which ends up usually about forty percent. (RIGHT – plus expenses) but a class action suit is a little bit different.

Pat: Well, okay, that's what's going on and it's about driving me nuts.

(Note: Months later I received a copy Debbie's medical report from my attorney and his letter stating that Debbie received all the proper care and the Heparin administered came from a safe source. There was no cause for a lawsuit.)

Tamara: Try to stay centered and only let this enter your mind when it needs to, when you need to address something. Let the rest go.

Pat: I wish Debbie could tell me what happened, because I wasn't there. I wish she could tell me.

Tamara: I'm seeing a pulmonary embolism. That's what I'm seeing.

Pat: That's what's on the death certificate. (HIT)

Tamara: I'm seeing a pulmonary embolism here. She did have an allergic reaction. I don't know if they did a toxic screen.

Pat: I don't think they did. And they should have, especially since she was in the emergency room two times in one week with hives.

Tamara: They really needed to do a tox screen on her. But it was some sort of allergic reaction. She went into toxic shock but the primary cause of death was a pulmonary embolism.

Pat: I know. It was first on the list.

Tamara: She was suffering from toxic shock and I don't know even if they had been able to get the trachea inserted in time how that would have affected her. I'm getting the pulmonary embolism was predominately the cause of death. It cut off oxygen to the brain and she —just stroked out. She definitely stroked out. So even if they had got her breathing again she would have never lived a normal life.

Pat: Thank you for that. (Crying)

Tamara: She would not have lived a normal life again. She would have had a long recovery from the stroke.

Pat: If she recovered.

Tamara: If she had recovered it would have been a very prolonged recovery and I'm not sure - okay - I'm seeing a lot of this was on her right side. I'm seeing a lot of stuff on her right side, right here (right side of the head) right here and right here. Her left side would have been devastated.

Pat: So it was a blessing?

Tamara: Yes, it was a blessing. And that she went that quickly and was asleep.

Pat: And she did. This was Thursday when she got up and said she didn't feel good. And I said to her, "Well, your medication is just about over with because you're going back to work the next week so let's see how you do." She'd been diagnosed with acid reflux and she was taking something for that and anxiety and she wasn't feeling any better. So I called the doctor and he said double up on the acid reflux medication. She was breathing hard, almost gasping by then. You see, her insurance wasn't good in Houston, so I said we needed to go back to Waco because if she was having an allergic reaction to some medications, she needed an allergist. I figured it was all the medications she had been given for the staph infection.

Tamara: I truly think that if they had done a tox screen they would have found out that all these medications were creating a toxic time bomb.

Pat: That's what they were doing.

Tamara: And they created the pulmonary embolism, the stroke, and it was like a Molotov cocktail in her body.

Pat: I should have just taken her straight to the emergency room here in Houston. I mean, I just should have called an ambulance. But ... but I never, never looked at her death as being a possibility, I never accepted any of this as life threatening.

Tamara: We won't because at certain ages we don't believe people can die. We don't believe people in their twenties and thirties can die, (Debbie was fifty-two), we don't believe six year-olds can die, but they do—every day. But it's not in our belief system to believe that.

Pat: I still can't believe it.

Tamara: But look at it this way, and this is hard to say, but she was probably better off leaving.

Pat: And she made her choice to go.

Tamara: She made her choice, she knew that. She knew that it was like stay or go, and in some ways she didn't want to leave you but she knew—okay, she knew that if she stayed and in consideration of the condition she would be in, she would have been such a burden on you.

Pat: And look what I've got here. She knew I was taking care of her grandmother. (Crying) I couldn't have done both of them. Her grandmother is like an empty box. I'd have had to put somebody in some kind of home because (Crying) Oh, dear God, well, I think we're through for the day.

Tamara: Well, I hope I helped you in some way.

Pat: I hope so, too.

Obviously, I was new at this. Was there anything I didn't tell her? Crap.

To say I was shaken would be to put it mildly. My mind was whirling as I drove over to Travis' party. I must have looked strange because a good friend of mine asked, "What's the matter?"

"I just had a reading by a psychic."

"Oh, my God!"

"You can say that again. She had a lot to tell me about Debbie, but I think I blew it."

"You need a drink," she said. And I did.

Twenty-One: A Closer Look

Katherine, beautiful in every way, was working part time now at her job. She was cheerful, tossing the tresses of her new blonde wig, laughing her longshoreman laugh, and fighting her way through chemo treatments. Paul looked drawn, his dark, curly hair worn long now, coiling softly around his neck. He'd lost weight, and his crystal green eyes, usually sparkling with humor, seemed clouded. Katherine said he'd been taking care of her like she was a princess. I'd offered many times to go over to help out but he said he had everything under control. I wondered. They were both in my prayers every day and I knew their angels were with them, helping and guiding them through this hateful time.

Paul told me the doctors were saying all the right things. The tests looked wonderful, they got it all, no signs of it recurring at this time, and they were amazed at her recovery. Then they dropped the piano on their heads. It could recur at any time, even pop up someplace else. So now they lived in terror of every little ache and pain she has as Paul rushes her to the doctor for another dreaded test. I know Archangel Michael will remove this fear and I thank God and his angels for her healing every day.

My angel cards were reminding me to detox my body and write, write, write. I needed to look into this Ion Foot Bath detox at Tranquility and I wanted to know more about this third eye thing. I started work on *Nixon's Women* that day. Paul wanted a first draft in two weeks.

I had a hum-dinger of a dream that night. Something about a party at a beach house and two engagement rings. Now, my angel cards have been giving me lots of relationship readings. Things like cupid, a new relationship, a new pet, and throwing in a wedding for good measure. Then this dream.

***

A flyer came in the mail that day entitled, "Enlarging Your Third Eye", a workshop at Tranquility by Ah-Shan. I called for a place in the workshop but went as the eternal pessimist, grumping and grousing.

It was a warm spring evening in May. I didn't record this workshop as it was a group thing. There were seven of us. We all had signed a disclaimer that stated we understood none of the instructors at the Center were passing as doctors. Okay by me and I signed away.

Ah-Shan is from Milan and he started off with a bang. "I don't believe in God," he announced. "Just astro force energy, protons, atoms, et cetera." Well, I kind of thought that was all part of God's plan, but what did I know? He launched his presentation and if anyone entered the workshop late, he just started over. He had tapes for sale and brochures up the Malian yingyang. The healing of animals was his specialty and, for us humans, cancer. I told him about Casey's tumor and he said he could guarantee it would not return and was offering a ninety-nine dollar special. The object of the workshop was to enlarge our third eyes so that we could absorb, see, and understand additional spiritual communications. We gathered our chairs in a circle.

The workshop began by Ah-Shan playing a relaxation tape. He then got on a mic to talk us into a deep meditation and up popped my colors, and my eye, which was blue metallic and about the size of a pea. Behind us, Ah-Shan moved about the room touching our shoulders and heads, giving our third eye a shot of light from some sort of a laser. Sure as hell, right there and then, my third eye tripled in size.

Then we partnered up. We each held a piece of jewelry from our partner and were told to hold it lightly centered in our right hands, per instructions. This exercise was to try and read our partner off their jewelry. We were to just say anything that came into our heads. I went back into my meditation and saw brightly colored flowers in a white rock garden. There was water and a bench with a red-headed lady standing close by. I told my partner what I was seeing. Not much, from her expression.

We took a break, held hands, and then went at it again. I told her I was seeing a dark brown wood bar, a party with friends and family having a good time. She told me when she was young they would have family reunions at their lake house and there was a big wooden bar against one wall and a bench in the garden. She didn't do so well when it was her turn to read me but I went home with my third eye larger than life and was quite pleased with the whole thing. One of the group asked Ah-Shan about weight control and he said to eat an apple and an orange every day and your metabolism will go sky high and you'll lose a lot of weight. I lasted two days on that one.

***

Mother's Day was upon me. AARP's chapter president called me and said they needed volunteers to take flowers to the nursing home we sponsored. They wanted to distribute flowers for all the mothers and could I help out on Saturday. Sure, I told her, not even recalling that the channeler had told me that she didn't know where they would come from but there would be flowers on Saturday or Sunday. It came in very strongly to her as she reminded me three or four times during my reading. When I'd left her, she'd called after me, "E-mail me about the flowers."

There were about ten to twelve of us volunteering at the home that day. We all wore our red AARP volunteer shirts and had a lot of fun visiting and giving out bunches of red carnations. After we finished, an older woman in a red volunteer shirt came up to me and said, "These red carnations are left over and you're suppose to take them home."

"Are you sure?" I asked.

"Oh, yes," she answered, "and thanks for coming today you made it so much easier."

I suddenly realized I hadn't thanked her for the flowers. I turned quickly to do so but she wasn't there. She was just gone. There was no one in a red volunteer shirt anywhere around me. I put the flowers out in Debbie's garden and e-mailed Tamara to tell her the flowers had arrived, special delivery.

Mother's Day I stayed low and quiet. My colors were different now. Instead of swirling, they were more defined as they move in and out. They circled, and in the middle of the circle there were shapes of metallic green and blue, sometimes even gold. My third eye was very large now and distinct. Were there tears on Mother's Day? Yes. Were there moments of deep despair? Yes. But the day was livable and I finished *Nixon's Women*.

Mom and I had lunch with Paul on Wednesday and I turned over the first draft to him. And then I had to sweat because I knew he'd be honest and direct. Paul pulls no punches when it comes to theater.

Twenty-Two: Sharing The Load

Perishable Theater, in Providence, Rhode Island, called late that next day to say they were interested in two of my plays. I like long distance calls from producers. If this happened, it would be in the summer and I'd sure enjoy a few days in that cooler part of the country.

Paul loved *Nixon's Women*. He could hardly wait to start saying all those dirty words. If you're going to write a play about Richard Millhouse Nixon, you'd better be prepared to use some language. We made arrangements to meet for a run-through of the first draft at a local *California Pizza Kitchen* tucked into a trendy uptown shopping center. Paul and I were joking around as we headed for our cars and he went into his, "I love America" Richard Nixon impersonation. He was flailing about, thumping on car hoods, as shoppers, taking one look, headed for the nearest shop door. Not that Paul noticed. He continued on until I said laughing, "Stop it, you're scaring people."

There was a meeting of Compassionate Friends that night. It was a small group; understandable since it was so close to Mother's Day, but there were lots of stories. One woman told two stories that she'd recently read. A minister had put his sleeping infant in an alcove just off the rectory while he gave his sermon. She was sound asleep in her carrier. His wife was visiting a cousin and he had arranged for someone to check on the child and, if she was found awake or unhappy, gave instructions for her to be taken to the child care facility. The minister delivered his sermon and went to retrieve the quiet child. The baby had passed.

The second story was about another minister who was at a church picnic at a small lake with his family. His wife was putting out food and he was watching their girls. A parishioner stopped to ask him something and when he turned around a few minutes, later both girls had drowned.

Next story. A young father was babysitting. He put his sleeping three month old son down in his crib and went back to his paper. When he returned a little while later to check on his son, he wasn't breathing. He was declared dead from brain damage when they reached the hospital. That was eight weeks ago. He could hardly talk.

On and on it went around the table. A twenty year old overdosed, another twenty-four year old had been killed on his motorcycle. The mother said she doesn't talk to God anymore. She retrieved his truck from where he parked it before he went riding with his friends and she just goes out and sits in it and cries. She lets no one near his things or his truck. His father went to use the boy's laptop one day and she went nuts. "No one touches Ronnie's things," she screamed at the terrified man.

By then we were all catatonic but the monitor tried to put a positive spin on it all. "What things are you doing for yourself?" she asked. It was my turn and, for the first time, I shared. I told them about Debbie's charity, her garden, going to the channeler, about not being able to get her urn open, and we all laughed at the thought of Debbie ending up in the Dust Buster. I talked about my deep pain and how I had started small when attempting to relieve it: having lunch with a friend, buying a best seller, getting a pedicure, trying to find a shred of good, and of opening the door to the smallest of opportunities, if only to aid my own healing. Carol Crandall wrote, "You don't heal from the loss of a loved one because time passes. You heal because of what you do with the time."

I was crabby and out of sorts the next day and nothing helped. Mom was up and waiting for me to fix her breakfast, the dogs were clambering to go out, there were pills to swallow, blood pressure to take, the morning paper to drag in, starting laundry—no wonder I was cranky. I read my Daily Word, did Angel Cards, and tried meditation. I prayed that God would replace my resentment with compassion. Am I angry because I think God took my girl and left me with an empty box to care for? Maybe so.

Later in the day I was thinking that I hoped Mom held up because I would really like to take that trip to the East Coast in the summer. I switched on the TV and there was a program on about James Van Praagh, the medium. I'd recently read that Shirley MacLaine said he was the real thing. I went to the computer and pulled up James Van Praagh and also a listing of top psychics in the country. Interestingly enough, most were located on the East Coast. I guess I'll just give this away, I thought, and see what happens.

I had to call Grant, my financial advisor, and up the ante on my annuity. I needed a little more money each month for expenses and prescriptions.

I sent flowers to Maddy, a friend who is in the hospital with leukemia, which she says she contracted while getting chemo for her breast cancer. She's a talented playwright and also a friend of Paul and Katherine. Did I tell them? No way. They have enough to think about. Let someone else deliver bad news. They did.

I'm turning over a lot lately: *Nixon's Women*, Katherine's recovery, my critters under the porch, writing a book, money, health, Mom, and Maddy. I've noticed that my thoughts regarding death are starting to change. I'd just seen on the news that Senator Kennedy has brain cancer. My first thought was what would a Kennedy reunion in heaven be like? What a party!

The other night in bed I felt a breath on my forehead. It was so strong it moved my bangs. I figured it was one of the dogs, as they sleep all over me and I can sometimes feel their breath on my arm or neck. I woke and found no dogs in my bed. "Hi, Debs."

I seemed to be doing better with my attitude regarding Mom and my morning rituals. That next morning I spread Deb's Tarot Cards out on the floor in front of me as per the reading. Nothing. There was only a jumble of cards on the floor.

I'm seventy now and what a time in my life to come alive. But I don't feel I'm near the end. Somehow I feel a beginning. Who knows what God has in store for me now that I'm beginning to find the truth. I feel the truth. I feel the other side and realize now that I've been writing metaphysical plays for thirty years. *Capote Tonight, Walk-In, Card-Carryin' Member, Breakfast with Billy*, all other-side stuff before I knew there was another side.

I woke at five a.m. the next morning and spent some quiet time in meditation with my angels and spirit guides. They were all there in their colors, blue, purple, a little red, lots of movement, lots of faces floating by, then a cruise ship, and animals. It was a real slide show. I whispered them a good morning and told them how much I'd like to talk to my guardian angel, whom I know is hovering about me all the time. No immediate reply. I kept reminding myself that this is a process. It's a slow and easy go, taking time to digest what I'm learning.

I signed up for a photography class. I got someone to stay with Mom for two hours; I really needed a break from her and the house. We'd had a run-in about the dogs. She fed the dogs a whole box of dog treats in two days. If I hid the dog treats, she fed them people cookies and Dukie was so fat, he waddled. Casey had a leg and hip problem and we had to keep weight off him. But Mom didn't get it, and fed them her food under the table at every opportunity. Maybe I was the one who didn't get it. She'd had a couple of spells lately, one in the grocery store and the other in a restaurant. I just had to watch her more closely. I could see she was failing and it depressed me. Would love and care be enough?

I seemed to be sleeping a lot and felt l like I'd been tired for a long time. I could almost anticipate losing Mother and feel the aloneness. It's hard to let go of her, but she's in her own world most of the time now and her conversation is very limited. If you ask her something her replies are sometimes off the wall.

"Is there anything special you'd like for breakfast?"

"There's a lot of water in the hallway. Did you know that?"

Or: "I have to run to Target for some printing paper. Want to go along?"

"No, I'm having lunch with Eleanor today so I'm taking my car."

She needed a lot of care by then. If I could manage to get her out to eat she'd complain the fork was too heavy or she didn't like the food. If I sent her to put on her pajamas, she'd return dressed in a fresh blouse, her pajama bottoms, and sneakers. I prayed for patience.

I called Pam to see how everyone was doing and during our conversation she told me a story. Years ago, when she was married and raising her family in Detroit, she was coming home from work and stopped at the grocery store. It was cold and raining hard. Mist was rising out of the street drains as it had been hot and humid that day and the sudden rain had quickly cooled the street. A few blocks from her house the car just stopped. No way would it start again. She got out, grabbed the two bags of groceries, and, on high heels, started for home. She got about half a block when she gave up and called out, "I sure need some help here; I'm never going to make it." Just then a car pulled up and a wizened, white haired woman, who could barely see over the steering wheel, rolled down the window and called out to her, "Get in the car, honey, before you melt." Desperate, she did and directed the woman to her house saying, "You know, you really should be careful picking up strangers." The woman just smiled and asked, "Do you believe in angels, honey?" "I sure do," replied Pam. "Good thing," replied the woman, because you've just met one." Pam got out of the car, and then turned to thank her. The driver and the car were gone. Not driving away. Gone.

Pam's nephew caught "Super Bug" in school off gym equipment about the same time Debbie was sick and had a terrible time. There was some discussion about removing his foot, but he was doing well now. I promised myself to go visit more often, but there's so many Debbie memories in Tomball. All they want to do is talk about her and old times until I want to run screaming all the way home.

A large shadow passed across the living room that night. It had been seven months since Debbie passed. I'd been having a hard time since May 29th. She seemed very close to me and I saw her sweet face so often that I'd just fold. I'd finished the last draft of *Nixon's Women* and the Christmas play for the church, *Jake's Christmas Bell,* that week and vowed to soon start the book. My angels and guides were whispering in my ear, *"It's okay, we're here, it's safe; turn on the computer and we'll do the rest."*

Twenty-Three: Stumbling Forward

Not placing in the Scriptwriters/Houston 10 x 10 Play Competition that year wasn't a surprise. The play I entered was really not competition material but just another stab at writing again. The winners were all new authors to me, which was a good thing; it meant new ideas and creativity. It was June and I went along day by day dreaming of Debbie, having thoughts and memories that made me "bubble up", my new phrase for wipeout. I fought a lot of fears every day, taking care of Mom, the book, dogs, house, and the reality of someday being left alone. Mom had to be given direction most of the time now. It was let's get in the car, out of the car, go this way or that. I'd have to have a firm grasp on her arm to lead her because I didn't think she knew where she was at times. It broke my heart. My neighbor stayed with her so I could attend a class or a meeting.

I really liked my photography class and was working with pictures on the computer when suddenly I felt Debbie close to me. She was like a warm blanket. That day my angel cards told me *Hello From Heaven* and *Work With Children*. I was beginning to look for "hello" signs, like the new brown and yellow Monarch butterfly darting across the backyard day after day, finding a dime near the day bed just after vacuuming the previous day, or a flutter of spider web across my face when walking the dogs in the cool of early morning. Some mornings I could see the sun begin to climb into the sky, turning it pink, blue, and purple, and I knew it was going to be glorious day.

I was in the living room straightening up one day when suddenly a strong scent filled the air. I knew it wasn't air freshener; it was an expensive perfume and it was familiar. I stood for several minutes as it washed over me. Then I remembered and walked into my bathroom. There was a small bottle of perfume in there that I had brought home from Debbie's house after she passed. I remembered one day telling her how good she smelled and asking what she had on. It was Celine Dion; her half full bottle was sitting on a shelf. I sprayed the air and, sure enough, that was it. These things comfort me, not frighten me, and I'm able to say out loud, "Hi, Debs."

***

Paul called today and we're doing *Nixon's Women* at Houston's first Fringe Festival in August. Next week we're going to look over the festival site, and Paul will begin casting and rehearsals soon. What a lift for both of us. We went to lunch and had a good metaphysical talk. We talked about dealing with the kind of stress we're up against. Katherine is well but neither of us can shake the fear of a recurrence. She's in my prayers every day. He told me about caring for his dad for three years while he was sick and he teared up. Men aren't supposed to cry—he thinks.

**

In meditation this morning my small inner voice said, *"Finish the Christmas play for the kids at the church and get busy on the book."* Nag, nag, nag.

**

A dream: I was alone in a movie theater. I had packages in my lap and around me. I was the third seat in and two people came and sat next to me. I couldn't see who they were but I suddenly realized that my left hand was being firmly held. I tried to shake it off but couldn't. I was frightened and woke up. I ate a whole box of Cracker Jacks and spent the rest of the day throwing up. Lay off the junk. I keep forgetting I'm not seventeen.

**

Mother had a spell and I had to take her to the emergency room; it was seven p.m. on a Friday and her regular doctor had closed up shop for the weekend. In the ER bed she began gagging and almost convulsing. She was very weak and I thought this was it. Her tests showed a urinary tract infection and they kept her overnight because of her age. By the time I took her home on Saturday, she was much better, but it was a "Your will be done not mine" sort of thing. I didn't know what was happening with her. If it was her time to cross over and be with our family, I'd make it okay and I knew I could handle it. She still had a little diarrhea when we got home and was very shaky, but she'd had a big shock to her system. In a day or so I noticed her mental capacity had slipped a little more. I suspected a mini-stroke, but by Sunday she had bounced back enough for church and an afternoon play, written by a friend of ours. The stress was beating me up and I was very tired. I slept a lot the next few days.

The next morning Dukie was having a fit out in the yard. I went out there and he had a fluttering bird in his mouth. Now it was my turn to have a fit. In response to my flailing about and yelling at him, he dropped the poor thing and it scrambled to the fence. I got him inside and settled down while Casey was half nuts thinking he was missing out on something huge. Going again into the backyard to see what could be done for the little creature, I went praying, "Lord, I don't want to handle this. What if it's seriously injured and I have to kill it?" I couldn't find the bird. I was very upset as I searched the yard twice, but it was gone. I'd like to think it recovered from its great fright and flew off. That's what I tell myself. Thank you, Jesus.

***

It was again time for a Compassionate Friends meeting. Siblings were invited to attend this month and there were a few scattered around the long table. There were butterflies and Kleenex on the table; butterflies because we all will emerge from our grief cocoons and Kleenex because there are always a lot of runny noses. Someone had brought homemade brownies, and there was hot coffee. Somehow spirits lifted and there was a smile or two around the table. It felt good. It was an interesting meeting. All of a sudden we started talking about strange things that had happened since our loved ones passed—that was *my* thing.

Having three grown children, three from a previous marriage, a police officer had had her tubes tied. After her daughter passed she had insemination done and it took the first time. She had twins. Well, the children are a couple months old now, and she was playing with them trying to get them to coo and such and, all of a sudden, she said, one of the twins looked behind her and started laughing. "I knew what she was seeing," she told us. "It was my daughter, Becky, and she felt very close to me at that moment."

The meeting continued around the table. There was the woman who still sleeps on her sofa that faces the door waiting for her son to come home, the same one that found the balloon. She cries so hard no one can understand what she's saying. Next were two women, I think a mother and a grandmother; neither could talk yet. Their loss was five months old.

Next, a mother whose son had committed suicide who sometimes hears the shower running. The woman on the other side of me lost her daughter a few days before I lost Debbie. She and her husband both talk to her daily and find things around the house, a favorite book, a bracelet found just lying around. They seem comforted.

I told the new people about my angels, about the turn signal in the car going off at the exact time Debbie passed, the dog's surgery, and the Mother's Day flowers.

Another woman talked about her son who had had a drug problem but had been clean for two years. He was in a program and was helping other kids kick their habits. He went over to his girlfriend's house one evening. Her mother found them both in her daughter's room. Both had O.D.'d. Since neither had insurance, they had been released to go home by a hospital just hours before.

Then the two young girls at the end of the table had my attention. They were in their late teens or early twenties. Both had lost their brothers, one to a motorcycle accident, the other to drugs. They were loud and disruptive during the meeting, abruptly leaving then returning several times. They looked rather worn and were both shoveling sugar into their coffee and brownies into their mouths as if there was no tomorrow. It didn't take a genius to figure out they were drugged out of their skulls. One was so eaten up with guilt she commented that she didn't care if she lived or died. She had taught her brother everything she knew about drugs, and even paid for the prescription drugs that killed him. He was fifteen. They didn't stay long.

One lady put together a scrapbook, another, a picture album. I still can't look at our pictures. We all agreed that sometimes the only thing you can do for a suffering child is let them go home to God. We are not in this thing alone.

***

The next week I took Mom to the doctors for a checkup. I asked him if we were looking at a nursing home in the near future and said he thought it wasn't too far off. His mother was in a nursing home. She has Alzheimer's. No wonder he pats my shoulder when I leave the office.

***

Why am I so damned tired all the time? That night I dreamed of Debbie but couldn't remember if she was there or if I'd just felt her. It was time to wake up.

***

Tim Russert, the host of *Meet The Press*, died today. I felt such a great loss as Debbie and I watched "Timmy" every Sunday morning that we were together. I was very depressed. Depression; maybe that's why I'm so tired?

***

Suddenly, it was June and Father's Day. Debbie and I didn't have good luck with fathers. Mine was gone when I was five and the next one was a drunk. Debbie's real father was really a peach until she was about five or six and then both of us went nuts. Me on diet pills, he—just nuts. After the divorce I tried again, married a Texan and moved to Houston. He left after seven years and never even said goodbye to Debs. She really liked him and it hurt her feelings but then, again, he hardly said goodbye to me. Forgive, yes. Forget? I'm still single. I'm beginning to think this planet earth is just a proving ground for how we handle all the crap that comes our way.

I'm learning how to give money away. Imagine, me, the Scrooge of Houston. It wouldn't surprise people if after I die they find the first dollar I made in my mattress. I'm keeping dollars in my wallet now and giving them away to street people. It really feels good. Also a woman at the church lost her mother who lives in Africa. She wanted so much to go to her mother's funeral so I donated some money through the church for her to go. An angel thought: *"If you share your own pain it will make another's easier."*

They're after me about that book again.

***

A dream: I went to the hospital for a flu shot and was diagnosed with throat cancer. I thought, I have to get home to make arrangements for Mom and the dogs' care. Thank God this was just a dream.

***

It was very hot the next day, close to one hundred two degrees. I finished the Christmas play and submitted others to various theaters around the country, then queried a publisher on *Capote Tonight*. Something would shake loose. I just knew it.

***

I approached my pastor the following Sunday and told her about the Christmas play I'd written for children and asked if the church would be interested in putting on a holiday play for the kids. Indeed they were and she wanted a copy right away. Then I went home and gave the dogs a bath. I was not their favorite person that day.

The church is making cloth dolls for a orphanage in Venezuela so the next Sunday morning, I packed up all of Mom's craft stuff and sewing supplies, i.e.; trims, buttons, glue, lace, thread, and whatever, and delivered two big boxes of it to the doll makers. I also delivered the Christmas play.

Dream: I was in a big auditorium and all my playwright friends were scatted about in the audience. I asked the person sitting next to me what was happening with the buzz around the room and at that moment, down the left aisle, close to the wall, came a young woman who looked like Debbie. She was dressed in a long stripped shirt just like the ones Debbie wore. I knew it wasn't her but it gave me a jolt and I ran to some of my friends and asked them to follow me up the aisle; that was the way the young woman had gone. We all ran up the center aisle and into the lobby and there she was, walking toward us. It wasn't Debbie but she looked and even walked so much like her that I knew I wanted it to be her. My friend said, "That's incredible." I woke up and went into the kitchen and cleaned the oven.

***

Years ago, when Debs was about thirteen or so and I was just divorced from her dad, we lived in a really nice apartment in Rochester, New York. It was a bright and sunny second story apartment; the living room windows overlooked the back yard and pool. It was a Saturday morning and Debbie was in her room doing homework while I cleaned the oven. This wasn't a built-in but a full stove and oven that slides into its designated space. Below the oven there was a drawer that pulled out where you could store pots and pans. I had pulled everything out and was diligently scrubbing away but I was having trouble reaching to the back of the drawer. I repositioned myself on the kitchen floor and stretched, pushing part of my shoulder half way into the drawer. I was uncomfortable but the drawer got cleaned. Then I suddenly realized I couldn't get out. I was wedged in there as tight as olives in a jar. Finally, I called Debbie and told her I was stuck in the oven. She got me out—but not before both of us wet our pants laughing.

***

The city came around the next day and trimmed my pear tree in the backyard. They needed to clear some of the branches from around the power lines and they gutted it. Debbie's garden was a mess. I stood out there crying as the city did their best to reduce me to rubble. I couldn't believe the damage. It was like I could hear the tree screaming and there wasn't a damned thing I could do about it. I tried to tell them to be very careful but none of them spoke English so I just gave up and stood there sobbing. I really think pixies and fairies live around Debbie's little

124

garden and that angels come often to visit them. There are always lots of butterflies and rainbows around, besides the birds, squirrels and a possum who visits at night. I spent the rest of the day cleaning it up and asking God to save that tree. He did because, you see, we are loved, protected and safe. And that included my tree. We won't go into the stock market.

***

Mom's specialist and I see a decline in Mom from visit to visit. He always tells me what a good job I'm doing caring for her. He had a trainee in his office the last time we were there and was asking me questions regarding Mom's health and care. "See," he remarked. "This is the difference between home and personal care as compared to a nursing home." She still can go with me many places like the movies and out to eat, a scriptwriter's meeting, and readings and plays on a Sunday afternoon. We can still take a ride to the mall or to a discount store for something or other. Some of the stores have a wheelchair with a shopping cart attached to the front, which is great. They get my business. She can't handle the riders. Mother has a haircut, manicure and pedicure once a month. As long as we can do this kind of thing, she's going to be home, where she belongs.

Twenty-Four: Angel Cops

Nixon's Women was coming together like a well organized jewelry box, although the rehearsals at Theatre One were intense. Outside the rehearsal hall where we were holed up, was a dance company in rehearsal for a show, and Paul, as Nixon, and Brenda Marsh, as Martha Mitchell, were going at it, so hard and so loud the dance instructor tapped on the door to see if everything was okay. It sounded like someone was being killed. There was lots of language flying around. We assured her all was well, that it was just a rehearsal and she went back to her students somewhat satisfied.

***

Dream: I was on a bridge outside a large city. As I looked down into the dark water below me I saw a huge fish surface. "Wow," I said. "Look at that! That big fish is eating the smaller ones." Then I suddenly fell into the water, but the water was more like Jell-O. It was thick, confining, and it was hard for me to swim toward the shore. It was more like I was pulling myself along. Suddenly, I noticed a pain in my right foot but I kept struggling through the goo and finally reached shore. My foot was swollen and bruised and I thought that big fish must have bumped me.

Then I woke up.

***

That next morning, I started writing the book. I only knew I wanted to not only tell my story but those of others. I liked to read stories so why wouldn't other people? Lots of stories had to be in this book: the "I'm not alone in this" stories, the "how I got here" stories. Above all, it had to be filled with good things: angels, faith, hope, and love. I knew I couldn't just dump on young parents that it may be thirty, forty or fifty years before they'd be reunited with a child. I wanted to tell them where their children are, what they're doing, and about a good that comes from all things.

I had to rebuild the months of Debbie's illness and death. Sometimes I could only do a couple of pages a day because I would be crying so hard, but I knew my angels were with me, encouraging me, helping me reach into myself to tell the stories so that another mother could one day say, "That's how I felt. I'm not alone in this."

***

Paul and I attended a Fringe Festival production meeting at the new Frenetic Theater in East Houston. It was still under construction and I mean under construction. No walls, no air-conditioning, no seats, no nothing. It was an old office building just west of downtown filled with dilapidated office furniture, broken file cabinets, stacks of torn out wallboard, an outboard motor, and just plain trash. They had cleared out a large area in the middle of this mess and put some benches and chairs around in a circle, placed an industrial fan to one side capable of blowing your clothes off and called the meeting to order. I had Mother with me and she wanted a softer place to sit than a bench. The fan was giving her a fit. The next thing I knew she was plowing through scaffolding and junk in a corner which held the remains of an old executive chair with the stuffing poking out. She looked like a refugee wandering around a disaster area. A young writer and I waded in to guide her out. No doubt about it, we were the entertainment of the day, but if she had fallen, that loony old lady would have given their insurance agent reason to keel over. It was the end of June and I had grave doubts that this theater would be ready for an audience in eight weeks, but what did I know?

***

The church was sponsoring a 4th of July picnic and I threw myself into volunteering to make potato salad and blueberry muffins. There were now small breaks in my gloom. Sometimes there was even a small rush of joy or a feeling of excitement for the future. Then one day I found some pictures Debbie had stored in my computer on a weekend she'd been home. There were some of her at one of her conferences and I completely lost it. A total wipe out.

I continued with my reading, prayer, meditation, angel therapy, and thanking God for his blessings every day. I felt I was in the process of breaking down the walls of my own resistance and making a small hole in that wall for moving forward, but towards what, I didn't know. I wished I could find some quiet in my disorganized soul or at least some peace in its chaos. *It's coming—it's coming.*

***

I was dealing my angel cards every day for guidance. They talked to me about daydreaming, welcoming a shower of abundance, looking to gentleness, taking back my power, looking into energy work, healing classes, and realizing this journey is a process to reaching my Christ consciousness. It's a breaking down, thawing out, and regrouping.

***

Dream: I was at one of my plays on opening night and Debbie was there sitting next to me. She looked beautiful and she was laughing and enjoying herself. Suddenly, I was up on the stage wandering among the actors as they tried to deliver their lines. They shortly got confused and started to flounder and lose their places. Slowly, I became aware of where I was and, leaving the stage, went to sit down, but Debbie was gone.

***

Working on the book was a chore. I'd known it would either have a healing effect or tear me apart. Right then, it was doing both. My journal was a great tool in bringing back my memories of all the things I had been doing and feeling in those dark days. The things I had buried that were now stalling me in the work. I asked God to send his angels to help me past this place, to help me to continue writing and sharing what was happening to me.

***

The 4th of July picnic at the church was a good day out. I took my promised potato salad, muffins, and talked about the Christmas play with the youth minister. On Sunday, Evelyn Crisp, our minister, had prepared to give a sermon on prosperity. Somehow, she got off on another subject and decided to stick with it—creativity. Creating a passion for the work and knowing that God, through you, can achieve whatever job is put before you. The sermon was right on target for me that day. It was time to put away doubts, fears, and insecurities. Was I concerned that God and his angels were not powerful enough to see this book to completion? No. My concern was about me. I was having trouble releasing from and reliving the experience of losing Debbie moment by moment. I wanted to run away from it. I wanted to pull the covers up over my head and say, "I don't want to go through this pain again. Stay away from me. Leave me alone."

Okay, angels, time to shake this off and move on. I fell back on what I knew: prayer and meditation. My colors swirled around me as I prayed: I need help, I'm stuck in my own fears, tears, and grief, and I can't seem to move ahead. A voice in my head spoke to me as clearly as if standing by my side. *Continue the research, tell the stories, and get out of yourself.* The cloud lifted and I went back to the computer that afternoon. My angel cops were on the job—as they always were.

Twenty-Five: And The Beat Goes On

The heat that July was wicked, the yard was going to hell, and both taps ran hot water. Day after day heat and humidity beat down on Houston with not a drop of rain in sight. I just kept digging in every day. Spiritual reading, writing daily in my journal, prayer, meditation, the book, angel cards with their *take a chance, don't expect perfection, Christ didn't* and *develop a passion for something.* I was thanking God for my blessings and trying to do one good thing for myself every day. Well, maybe not every day, but I was sure getting out: Scriptwriter's meetings and a take your lunch holistic workshop at church on Wednesdays. The economy was going to hell along with my annuities, but I was loved, protected, and safe.

At the July meeting of Compassionate Friends interesting things happened. A year after Garrott crossed over, his parents had friends visiting who spent the night. They slept in their daughter's room as she was away at school. At about three a.m. both husband and wife woke at the same time. They saw Garrott at the end of the bed, surrounded by a blue light. They knew it was Garrott and so did his parents as the guests told their story, stating they'd recognized him by the blue corduroy coat and brown Chinos he always wore. He didn't say anything, he was just there. The guests quickly packed and left, visibly freaked out.

Carla told of her son who had been clean of drugs for two years. He'd overdosed at the rehab center a few weeks ago. He was rushed to the hospital and later released. He died a few hours later in his own bed. Now, Carla and her husband had been separated for eight months before their son died. She was in such bad shape her husband moved back into their house, but not for long. He'd moved out again the following Sunday. Carla's eyes were dead.

There was a mother, Lea, and father, Carlos, there that night with their fourteen-year-old daughter. Two weeks earlier, their seventeen-year-old daughter, Alma, had complained of stomach pain. Lea took time from work the next day and took Alma to the doctor, but their regular doctor wasn't there that day and another doctor was standing in for him. He gave Alma a quick exam, ran a couple of tests, and wrote a prescription to relieve what he diagnosed as a slight gall bladder attack, then sent her home. She had an uncomfortable night and in the morning when her dad asked how she felt she told him she still hurt a little but was better. "Still, she asked, "would you take off work today and stay home with me?" He did, as her mom confidently went off to work and Alma went to take a shower. Carlos heard Alma fall. He managed to get her out of the shower but she was by that time delirious. She died in his arms on the bathroom floor.

Alma had been an honor student and already had accumulated thirty-five thousand dollars in grants for her college education. The autopsy showed that gall stones had ruptured her pancreas. Even their family doctor screamed negligence. The relief doctor was fired and a lawsuit was pending. But Alma is physically not with us here on earth any longer.

Carlos had more of his story to tell. He said he couldn't help crying all the time, especially at work. Mostly, he was just nicely ignored as tears ran down his face. All his coworkers knew what had happened and gave him a wide berth. There was a young man, Robert, who worked with Carlos. Robert called his mother every day. Carlos reported that it was pitiful how Robert talked so unkindly to his mother on the phone day after day—but he never mentioned it to Robert. He had his own troubles. The next day Carlos walked out to his truck on his lunch break and was sitting there crying when Robert approached. Carlos said he noticed Robert in the rear view mirror when he stopped about ten feet from the truck. He stood for a few minutes then came around to the truck door. "Carlos, he said. "I just saw your daughter sitting next to you here in the truck. She had her hand on your shoulder." Stunned, they both returned to their jobs. That afternoon Robert called his mother and apologized for the way he'd been talking to her, for his many hurtful actions of the past, and on the spot turned his whole life around. "I didn't cry so much after that," Carlos recalled, "and Robert was a different person."

Four years ago this month two eighteen year old boys were involved in a car wreck. The speeding and reckless driver left the accident on the run, leaving his passenger to die alone in the car. He was apprehended by the police and went to jail for four years. After three and one-half years he was paroled for good behavior, despite his drug and reckless driving record. "He's out. My son is dead. He'll never come home again," cried the broken mother from across the table. Her hooded eyes had dark circles and she was a rack of bones. She kept pulling her sweater tighter around her body although it was very warm in the room.

***

I believe that the grief process can either bring a couple closer together or break them. Do fathers bury this horrible grief deeper and, therefore, function at a higher level than a mother? I don't know, but a grieving mother screaming at a husband, "I must have loved our child more or you'd be suffering like I am," doesn't seem to answer this question. Or the proverbial, "He's been gone six months now. When are you going to get over it?" If our grief is not of primary concern to God, why would He have promised to send us a Comforter? He has, loved ones. They are all around us.

Grief in many forms surrounds us all. The loss of a job, moving to a new city, divorce, losing a valued piece of jewelry, even a misplaced book or one not returned can shake our foundation. A quote from *Out Of Africa* by Isak Dinesen, "Does he lend out his books?" She asked. "Not anymore," he replied. "He lent a friend a book and didn't get it back. I asked him if he would lose a friend over a silly book and he answered, "No, but he did."

I don't lend my books, either. I either give one away or buy one for a friend.

What about the grief we feel regarding sickness in ourselves or others or losing a caregiver? I'm very concerned about being sole caregiver to my ninety-two-year-old mother. Could she outlive me? What would happen to her? God knows. And He does.

***

I received a surprise this morning. When I came back from walking the dogs I found a pair of underpants in the driveway. I know they weren't there when I left because I looked to see if the paper had been delivered and it hadn't. I don't even think they were mine. Have I told you angels have a sense of humor?

***

A week later I started to go through my and Debbie's jewelry, keeping what I wanted and putting the rest in a shoe box to go to the church's resale shop. I did very well until I found a picture of her that had been tucked away. It was all over for me that day.

***

The stock market was down again but I was giving all that to God. The only thing I knew was that my days didn't change. My bills were paid and groceries were in the cupboard. I felt good physically, but I was just so damned drained most of the time, falling asleep in my chair every day.

I sent *Nixon's Women* and a collection of short plays in for copyright registration a few days later and delivered my photo and bio to Paul for submission to The Fringe Festival so they could print up the programs.

Having lunch with Paul a week later I noticed he looked worn out and distracted. I knew he was worried about Katherine's cancer returning. I gave him a blue glass angel to give to her with a candle behind—so she'd light up.

Later, at home, I dropped off to sleep in my chair. I had on one of Debbie's bracelets and my arm fell over the side of the chair. Duke aggressively pushed my hand aside as he moved and sniffed the bracelet. Then he gave it a lick and went on his way. I believe he knew it was Debbie's and was reassuring himself she was still around.

Casey chased a cat the next morning on our walk and came home limping. I called the vet for an appointment. Mom also had a bad day and I had to make a doctor's appointment for her. I gave both dog and Mom a pain pill. Me, I had a wine cooler.

There was a storm in the Gulf—Dolly—headed for Corpus and the stock market plunged again. I was putting lots of prayer into the situation. I retrieved the mail and there were my bank and annuity statements. I'd lost thirty-two thousand dollars in the market so far this year. I balanced my bank statement and found I had forgotten to enter my last Social Security check. Thank you, God, for my prosperity.

***

In meditation today my colors were bright blue and gold with sharp metallic purple flashes. Inside the metallic flash I could see objects and then a glowing angel drifted across my vision, very small, very white.

***

It started to rain thanks to Dolly, but by the next morning I knew we'd soon be back to normal—and drought. Going out to my car that afternoon I found the small, golden angel that Debbie had kept in her car. It was in my beverage carrier. You figure it out but while you're doing that, look for the joy. It's there, I promise you.

Twenty-Six: Another Voice

July was almost over and I decided to take a day off. I got a sitter for Mom, went to church, and then over to Tranquility. I was going to try an Ion Foot Bath to clear out nasty toxins from my body, and then have a tarot card reading. It was a beautiful afternoon and there were a lot of things going on there: it was Psychic Fair day. Since my angel cards were frequently telling me to detox, I was ready to try the foot bath, but I also had my eye on reflexology, ear candling, and palmistry. For several weeks now I'd been getting angel thoughts regarding a past life reading, but I didn't think I was ready for that yet.

The foot bath was relaxing and revealing. A short haired, bustling lady named Diane came and collected me. After some preparation of the bath and cleansing of my feet, I slipped both feet into the bath. She told me that as the toxins were released from my body the water would change color. Sure enough, after about ten minutes the water changed to a dull yellow, then to orange. After about fifteen minutes it was green. In a few more minutes it turned black. I was amazed. My feet were dried, creamed, and my shoes slipped on. Diane told me it was a good session. In other words, I was full of it. I could have told her that. I had a cold drink and then went in to see my tarot reader. The results are as follows:

Tarot Reading with Marleen

Tranquility Spiritual Center

July 28, 2008

Setting up recorder:

Pat: I hope I get this right. It's moving. Let's get this recorder right in front of you because I don't have anything worthwhile to say anyway.

Marleen: (Laughing) All right. I know I've never read for you?

Pat: No.

(Handing over the cards)

Marleen: These are yours. I don't care how you shuffle them but shuffle them really well so you don't pick up the last person. What I do is a quick spread and tell you what I see coming up. That way I can connect with you. You can stop me if something is not resonating with you and you can reshuffle or I can shuffle for you. I don't usually have that problem but I do sometimes with men more than anything. And then we'll go into any questions you may have so be thinking about your questions while your shuffling and I'll be quiet for a second and let you do your thing. Shuffle them until they feel right.

(I shuffle)

Pat: They feel right.

Marleen: If they don't let me know because I'm not convinced you did it enough but we'll see. You're an Aquarian. (HIT) What's your birthday?

Pat: January 31st.

Marleen: Okay. Is there anybody in your life? You're not married. (HIT)

Pat: No.

Marleen: Okay, one male coming up. I'm not convinced you shuffled enough. I'm not feeling it.

Pat: Okay, I'll re-shuffle.

Marleen: Just kind of focus on it, because you were busy talking with me last time.

(Re-shuffle and giving the cards back. There was a pop up and Marleen said that sometimes she likes to read the pop ups to see what comes out. Sometimes they tell stories.)

Pat: How long have you been doing this?

Marleen: Since 1986, off and on. I came out in 2006 and opened my own business on line.

Pat: I'll be darned. Okay, let's try again.

(She spread out the cards.)

Marleen: This is telling me that there's been a lot of things in your past that you've had to let go of. Right now, in the upright position, is the Page of Swords. This card tells me that this is a streamline card for you. It's telling me that there are things that you may be cutting out of your life right now, things that you need to handle. This is about getting rid of things. I call it the spring cleaning card. This could even be about people in your life. Sometimes there might be people needing to leave as well. So this is you coming through things and this might be that you're thinking about redoing some things in your life. It's a remodeling card, even.

In your outer world, what I see right now is money coming from outside sources, so this is assistance for you. So this is coming in right now or you're waiting for something to come in, but it tells me there is money coming from outside.

Okay, this is your wishes and dreams card, and it's coming up reversed so it's telling me you're waiting for something but it may not be moving in a timely fashion and may be a disappointment for you. So it's telling me you may be feeling let down. Are you having feelings of let downs at all?

Pat: Not any more than usual.

Marleen: (Deals another card) Okay, okay, you're an Aquarian. The moon's coming up beneath you, so what I'm getting is on an emotional level. What I'm getting right here is emotional and you've been through a lot in your life. This is past also. Have you come out, or come through it? I think you're in a place right now that I feel like you're looking ahead and saying, "Okay, where do I go next? What's the next step for me?"

(Deals another card) Now this is your work card. Are you working right now?

Pat: No. I work at home but not out.

Marleen: Okay, that's fine. It doesn't matter where it is, it's still working. But this is telling me—and it's coming up reverse, so this is how you manifest money in your life. So this is telling me that maybe your work isn't bringing you what you truly want in life and maybe you feel like it's really stuck right now and maybe you're thinking about making a change there. But I'm feeling as it's reversing that there's a change coming in what you do, or maybe looking at a different location or something. But there's a definite change coming your way on how you earn your income.

(Deals another card) This card is telling me you're not resting well?

Pat: Off and on.

Marleen: Okay, this card tells me that maybe you need to meditate more. This card can also tell me that there's some unsettled stuff, like when you go to bed at night you lie in bed thinking about things and that's when everything hits. This is a quiet the mind card. It's coming up reversed, and it tells me you have some unsettling things right now. You've got some Swords coming up. You are the Queen of Swords, so this tells me that you'd rather think about or analyze than feel. Feelings are not an Aquarian's forte. And this is telling me again that you're going to do something right now. I've got these two cards here telling me that you are ready to handle something. I'm feeling that this is an impatience card and it's telling me that you're a streamliner and want to cut through something again. You've had this come up twice already.

(Another card) Okay, this card is your work again. Sometimes it deals with real estate, too, but this indicates something is not going right. I don't know if its real estate deals or something else. I feel that there is a career change for you. Or that you're looking at doing something different around your work.

(New card) Okay, new adventures for you. This card can sometimes be—you're getting ready to make changes. This is all I know. This is your new adventure card coming up. New beginnings for you. Sometimes you can be standing on a ledge and this can be a little scary because you're so afraid you're going to fall you don't give yourself a chance to try. But this card can mean travel ahead for you. So you may be planning a trip or it can also be new beginnings. So I feel like when I'm looking at this that you have some big changes coming up and you're beginning to look at things differently and it's time to get rid of stuff that doesn't really work for you, that kind of thing. Because you're willing to bring in new energy and I feel like you're an innovative person and have a good mind, sharp, always thinking about new ways of doing things. Definite changes coming for you.

So do you want to go on from here? Does this resonate with you at all? Do you want to go on?

Pat: Sure, let's go on.

Marleen: Do you have any questions? Do you want me to keep throwing?

Pat: Yeah, let's go on.

Marleen: Okay. Well, this right here is telling me that one thing that is really important to you is balance. You're a person who likes a lot of balance in life. I don't think you deal well with change of anything, but this is kind of who you are. This, Pat, right here, is telling me that this is a list of opportunities and I don't know why and it looks like there's a lot of things that might be presenting themselves to you right now or might be coming in because of your past hurt. So in other words, you think that what's in the past might affect how you handle what's coming up. It's like this is always a carpet of opportunity but don't let your past dictate your future. I feel this is the message in this. Because of past hurts or past disappointments I feel like you might have a tendency to let feelings slip back in time and stop you. Have you done that? Look back in time and say I wish I would have done that?

Pat: That's right

Marleen: Okay. I think there's an old tape running in you that keeps that from happening. That's an Aquarius. You have three cups here and cups rule emotions. And I know Aquarians well. I lived with one for four years. They don't like dealing with anything. If it's ooey, gooey, or messy in any way they would rather pick up the carpet and sweep it under rather than deal with it. But I see here that—I almost feel like you should sit down and have a good cry or something and then move on. It feels like something you haven't quite handled. Maybe a past hurt or something and I have a feeling that it's something that has kept you from truly moving on. It feels like something is getting in the way of your inspiration to yourself. I know that sounds peculiar, maybe, but do you know what that is?

Pat: (Nods)

Marleen: Okay. Because I feel that this is your spiritual connection to yourself and I feel like there is this big disappointment in your life. Maybe like you were waiting for something to happen and this is a messenger card and this is emotional. It's not a messenger, like the DH truck showing up at your house. This is like something like you expected from someone. Like someone let you down. Like I see emotionally you are unsettled but I think you're in the process right now of working through this. I feel like you're letting go here. But I really feel that this almost cut you off from experiencing a lot of joy in your life. I don't know what *it* is. You're not married, right?

Pat: Yes.

Marleen: Okay. Were you married ever?

Pat: Yes.

Marleen: Okay. Divorced.

Pat: Long, long time ago.

Marleen: Let me say this: your opinion of marriage isn't so hot.

Pat: Probably true. I don't think I'll ever marry again.

Marleen: Okay. Actually, you know what this card is telling me? You're a person who can make your own fun, so get out there and do it, because you know how. I think for you it's like turning on a light switch. You just have to do a little shifting up here (points to her head) and you may do a little healing in dealing with the stuff that you've shoved away and you haven't dealt with it. But I really feel that you could just step outside today and make up your mind to make the change and it's that simple for you. I don't feel that you need like five years on a psychotherapist's couch or anything like that. You just have to do a shift.

(Another card) What do you do? You're creative.

Pat: I'm a writer.

Marleen: Oh, you *are* a writer. Well, is your writing struggling or something like that?

Pat: Yeah. I'm a playwright and I'm just recently made a switch to a novel and it's slow going.

Marleen: Okay, because this is kind of what your cards have been telling me. Are you waiting for some money to come in? I don't know how this writing business works. Is there some kind of literary agent or anything like that?

Pat: No, nothing like that. Nothing coming. Just do this book. Then we'll see.

Marleen: Okay. No wonder I see change in your career. So you're not changing completely, but the way you do it.

Pat: Yes. This is a whole new concept in what I'm doing.

Marleen: Okay. Because I'm getting some funny things about money which is telling me that money comes to you from an outside source. But right now I see frustration with your career in manifesting money, so I could see if you're in a shift right now.

Pat: Money is not a problem. Not that I have a lot of money, but I'm okay.

Marleen: But I'm sure getting the career shift in regard to your job, because I do see outside assistance for you. This tells me it's going to come in from other places. What kind of writer are you?

Pat: Uh, playwright. But right now I'm writing a book on grief.

Marleen: Oh, really.

Pat: Yep.

Marleen: Maybe that's why. You know that's really interesting. One of the things I see is maybe as you write this book on grief you're feeling some things.

Pat: I sure am. That's why it's so slow going. I spend so much time crying.

Marleen: Okay, that's interesting. Because I think the things we write about are about issues to some degree. (Cards are spread out all over the place now.) Anyway, this has a lot to do with your work and I think you're wanting to move it forward.

Pat: I do, but I can only handle only so much a day.

Marleen: I can imagine that would be tough. No questions? Because I'm getting from this card that you want to grow. Also I think what happens with you is that—this is your heart card coming up—and you are a High Priestess. What happens is that when you get to impasse where you're maybe having an epiphany, and I almost feel like that's when you have the stall-out. It's like I feel like you're having a lot of feelings right now on this.

Pat: I am.

Marleen: Because I feel that when you're writing it's uncomfortable for you because you hit something that resonates and that's where the block is. Okay. This book, now I'm stuck on this book for some reason. I see this book making you a lot of money. (Laughing)

Pat: Fat chance, but whatever comes in it's all going to a charity set up in Debbie's name.

Marleen: Good, if you're okay with it, then, you know, I guess it's okay because what I see is in trying to move forward with this. It looks like this is a moving card. You're not physically moving are you?

Pat: No.

Marleen: Okay, then its work. Either home or work. But this is telling me—and its coming up reversed so it's hard for you to move this forward. No questions?

Okay, did you ever have a Sage in your life? Maybe a Sagittarius, Aries or Leo, a past husband?

Pat: No wise old men but wait a minute, now. I had Scorpios, two Scorpios.

Marleen: Oh, no wonder. You had two Scorpios? No wonder you're different.

Pat: Yeah, and I went back for more with one of them.

Marleen: Well, good. They're such great lovers, but they're so full of shit.

Pat: Oh, God, tell me.

Marleen: (Laughing) Okay, just so you know that I'm not telling you anything you don't know because your marriage card is coming up divorced. And if you told me anything was happening I'd have to tell you: run, this is not it.

Pat: I'm not a bit surprised. I'm not going to say that there might not be a friendship but—and I may even live with somebody.

Marleen: You see, I'm kind of wondering if you haven't had somebody, because there's a King of Wands, so this could be a friendship, but it's not going to go anywhere, I'll tell you that much. It might be a dinner person or something like that, but I was kind of curious as to why he pops up in the middle of this, because on either side of him, look, no marriage, no marriage. Do you know anyone, a friend right now?

Pat: Yes, but just friends. Also I'm caring for my mother right now and that's a commitment and a half.

Marleen: Okay. Well, here's your future/past. You know, you're embarking on your future right now and what I feel is this book is what you're supposed to be doing because, look, this is your judgment card. This shows me that angels are beckoning to show you this is your life path card. There's a lot of fear coming up with this. You have a Devil card right next to your past so I think there's something deeper going on as you process this work. I don't know what this is for you, but I feel this is one of the biggest things you have ever done.

Pat: I think it's going to be.

Marleen: Big. Big. I think this is going to be very big for you and you are possibly facing skeletons maybe and this is why you're struggling with this so much.

(And now, again, I couldn't shut up.)

Pat: My daughter died.

Marleen: Oh, I'm so sorry.

Pat: That's why I cry all the time but ... (Crying)

Marleen: Is this recent?

Pat: Eight months ago, but I'm getting a lot of help. My church and a grief group, Compassionate Friends and I saw—first of all I said I've got to go because I have to know that I'm not the only one this has happened to. And so I went to a meeting and I saw the anguish. That's the only word I can come up with. And all of a sudden, the book came to me in meditation through my angels, and I thought maybe it could help people through this. Maybe someone will read it and think, well, I'm not the only one. I went through all this but in doing it, I'm up to the fifth chapter, I have to go through the whole thing. And I'm back in that hospital room again and I'm seeing the things I've have shoved away and now it all comes back to me in the writing. It's like a movie and I'm watching it all over again.

Marleen: No wonder you're really struggling. But you know, I think—I know this sounds funny, but I think and I know you're not there yet, but as time goes on you're going to see that this is a gift your daughter gave you.

Pat: I think so too, because we have to start to find something good in this.

Marleen: Yes, you don't want her life to be in vain. My sister died, so I've been through this in my family, but a long time ago. My mother has never gotten over it.

Pat: I won't, either. You never do. You never do.

Marleen: She goes on. And this year I was at a party and one of my closest friend's son was shot and killed right there at the party. He was fourteen. This happened last September and it shook all of us forever, especially his mother. They were fooling around with an antique rifle that they thought was just a relic and one of the boys took it off the wall and was playing around with it and the gun went off.

Pat: It was loaded?

Marleen: Well, they say that there must have been a bullet lodged or stuck in it that nobody ever knew about or checked because it was an antique and just a fixture on the wall. It was horrible. We were out in the country and Life Line couldn't land because it was wooded. It was one of the worse nights of my life.

Pat: He passed right there?

Marleen: Yes. It got him right in the heart. He was fourteen years old. Anyway, have you ever met with a medium? There's a woman who lives up in New York now. She used to live in Houston. Her name is Myra Brannigan. She's very good. Do you have internet? I have to tell you I took my friend to her when she was here and it was extremely healing for her. Myra is an amazing medium. It brought my friend so much comfort to meet with her. She does do phone consultations. I don't think on a grand scale her fee is outrageous. I don't know if this is something that would help you or not.

Pat: Well, I really go into all this. I read lots of books, John Edward, Shar Margolas.

Marleen: Andrew George is amazing, as well. Andrew has written a lot of books and is one of the first mediums that came out. He's also in New York.

Pat: There's a lot of mediums in New York. In the back of Edward's book is a listing of recommended mediums and a lot of them are in New York.

Marleen: I have to tell you I think Myra's better than John Edward. She doesn't ask any questions or fish for names. She just goes in and starts. I know two people who have had phone consultations with her and both were very pleased. I know your daughter would be very much with you.

Pat: My minister said the other day that when you come into new awareness you break apart and then you have to go back together. But there's a piece missing; will always be a piece missing. Debbie was my only child, which makes it worse.

Marleen: Oh, sure, I understand.

Pat: You know, my mother lives with me and she's ninety-two. And I was as much as you can be prepared for her passing. I was prepared for her because of her age and the Alzheimer's and everything else and I was sure that was the way it was going to be and then this with my daughter came and hit me out of the blue.

Marleen: Was she sick?

Pat: She got that Super Bug, a virus and staph infection.

Marleen: You're kidding. How did she get that?

Pat: She was cleaning while she was at work. She was a drug and alcohol counselor for kids at TYC, and with all the scandal last year they were closing down facilities and moving some of these kids to her facility and she was supervising the cleaning of the dorms. But she just didn't supervise. She dug in and helped and we think that's where she picked up the infection.

Marleen: A friend of mine's son got that. He had a minor surgery and got it in the hospital and was dead three days later.

Pat: Well, Debbie beat it. Oh, God, she had three surgeries and, oh, it was horrible. And then she beat it and she came home. She was going back to work the next week and she got up and said, "I don't feel good." For the next few days she didn't feel any better, and Saturday I said, "You're going back to the hospital in Waco." And she was gone Monday. It was blood clots.

We were both in tears by then. My time was up and we parted close friends, friends that had shared something very important. I went home and took a nap. When I woke I felt refreshed. My concerns about Mom and my frustration seemed calmed. Finding the eggs in the freezer, the coffee pot cord pulled out of the wall every morning, feeding the dogs her meals under the table were now just "stuff."

I'm ready for *Nixon's Women*, the Fringe Festival, the Christmas play, and whatever, I said bravely while backing off a cliff.

July came to an end with me doing regular chores, reading, writing, praying, and meditations. I was still very tired and often fell asleep in my chair watching TV. I was peaceful at times now and the resentments of taking care of Mom full time were lifting. I care for her now because I love her, not because I feel obligated to.

***

It was early August and I had another dream. Debbie and I were driving someplace, laughing and talking together. I looked at her, thinking how good this was to have this closeness again. She was her old self, dressed in jeans and a bright, multi-colored shirt. Her complexion was smooth and glowing. I said to her, "This is so good. I've missed you so much." She just looked at me, smiling, but she didn't answer so I said it again, "Debbie, I've missed you so much." Then the dream faded and I woke up.

The one thing I've noticed about these dreams is that they're different from other dreams. Other dreams slip by me. I wake up thinking, wow, I was dreaming about Brad Pitt and it was a great dream but it quickly fades away from memory—if it's remembered at all. Visitation dreams stay. They are vivid, meaningful, and every detail is remembered upon waking. Sometimes crying, sometimes feeling warm and blessed, but remembering. In July in Houston, one also wakes feeling hot and sticky.

# Twenty-Seven: A Conversation With Heaven

One day in early August I was in the drug store/post office substation when I saw on one of the shelves a crystal cube with a shimmering white angel inside. She was beautiful. I instantly bought and brought her home. If I had thoughts of giving her as a gift, they soon left and she found a home sitting on the window sill of my study. The next morning as I was working on the book, I left the room to get a cup of coffee and when I returned I noticed a small but vivid rainbow reflected on the carpet. Where on earth did you come from, I thought. Then I investigated and noticed when I placed myself between the window and the rainbow it dissipated. By then I was on my hands and knees following the sun's rays. Sure enough, it was the morning sun shining through my crystal angel on the windowsill and casting a rainbow on the carpet. That's when I heard the bell. Not a bong, bong bell, but with a different sound, like a soft tinkle.

"Hi, Debs, and my angels," I called out. "I'm on to you now."

A few days later, on Sunday, the temperature was on its way up to one hundred and two degrees, the hottest day I could remember in Houston, a real record setter. The lawn and flowers were fried. There was no sense in even trying to water as it evaporated before it hit the ground. Mom was having a good day and my next door neighbor stayed with her so I could hang out in my cool church service and take in an afternoon play. It was time for the FOO, the Festival of Originals, a contest for one-act plays by local playwrights presented annually by Theatre Southwest. Four of my friends had won slots. It was great fun being with everyone for the afternoon and, I hate to say it but, I thoroughly enjoyed being there without having to care for Mom.

Tuesday, Hurricane Eduardo was churning in the Gulf. Casey chased a cat and then could hardly put his right hind leg on the floor. I said the same thing about booze as I'd said about giving up coffee. Maybe I gave them up too soon. No coffee, maybe that's why I'm so tired.

Again, with my neighbor staying with Mom, I took Casey to the vet. I was petrified. It was too soon. I was sure I was looking at another loss. Two years earlier he'd had to have surgery on his left leg. A tendon was damaged and he couldn't put that foot on the ground, either. I cried all through the examination expecting to be told he would have to be put down any minute. Not so; same problem as the left leg. Surgery was scheduled for the following Friday. I picked him up on Saturday and hand fed him scrambled eggs for two days, then spooned ice cream into his bowl and brought it to him. He hobbled around three legged and it was a while before he ventured putting any weight on that back leg.

In a few days he was doing better but it was tricky getting him outside with the limp. He still couldn't put his right hind foot down on the ground, but was perfecting the three-legged poop.

Mom was wandering the house like a lost soul but Eduardo brought a good steady rain and the heat broke. About a week later Casey jumped up on the bed to sleep with me and I knew we'd gotten him through another round. There was no sign of the cancer.

I spent time gathering up what was left of Debbie's stuff in the garage and some things of my own for the resale shop. I put the boxes and Mom in the car and drove to the church. While I was there I wanted to check on the Christmas play and to tell them that, because of nursing Casey, I didn't think I'd be at the Wednesday lunch workshop. Delivering the boxes, I drove across the parking lot to the church building. With the air pumping, I left Mom in the car and ran in to see Karla Robinson, who was in charge of the Unity Youth Group. Yes, they were going to do the play. I left her office after telling her about the jewelry I'd just dropped off. On the way to the church exit, I passed Nancy Quinn's office. She was doing the Wednesday a.m. workshop that week and I stuck my head in her door to tell her about the dog and that I probably wouldn't be there on Wednesday. I later learned that Nancy was a board member of the church, a registered nurse, has a master's in psychology, and is a hypnotist and medium.

Before I could speak, she looked up and said, "Glad you stopped by. I was just talking to Debbie." I was struck dumb and just stood there in her doorway. I'd heard we had a medium in the church. I'd seen this woman around but didn't know her.

"Come on in and sit down," she invited. I did, slowly lowering myself into the chair across from her desk while she commenced to give me a reading on the spot.

"You have a lot of questions," she said. "We'll try and answer them. Shoot."

This is what followed: I would ask a question and she would tilt her head to the right side, listen, and answer. She told me that Debbie was happy and had made the transition to heaven very quickly. That she was working with small children, wearing bright colors, and having a ball.

I told her about the blinker going off the night Debbie passed and she answered cheerfully, "Goodbye, Mom." She was smiling.

Nancy told me the heavy, close feeling I'd experienced in the car that night was Debbie's energy staying around for a while, seeing I got home safely. She told me that Debbie had come out of her body long before she passed and that she chose to pass alone because of our strong bond. I would have fought her passing. She went on that Debbie couldn't breathe because of the liquid in her lungs and that her whole body had shut down: kidneys, bladder, and then, of course, the blood clots.

I asked, "Did Debbie know she was going to die?"

Tilting her head almost to her shoulder, she said, "Yes, but she didn't tell you because you wouldn't have accepted it." She was above watching the whole thing and she just told me, "Who would want to stay in that body?"

I told her Debbie had been morbidly obese and she said, "I know, but not anymore."

She went on but it seemed as if we had somehow lost Nancy during the conversation and Debbie was speaking directly to me. Nancy was talking, but it was Debbie's voice I heard. "Mom, this is important. Keep writing. Angels are helping you. Grams and the book are life missions for you. And don't forget on your 'grief' research the Alzheimer families. Your return to Unity will only help your writing. There's no limit on anything in heaven so I can divide my energy between you and the children I'm caring for. We have a lot of family behind us. Look into this."

I asked her, "Could you have survived?"

"No, she answered, "nothing could have been done. But you're not taking care of yourself, Mom. Just because I'm not there physically, you have to live on. Okay, I have to go but I'll see you later." That was the last thing she'd said to me in the hospital the day she passed.

When I got back to the air-conditioned car, Mom was asleep. I drove home frazzled.

The next day, August 7, 2008, I wrote in my journal: A year ago the nightmare began when Debbie first got sick and it's been an ongoing journey. Yesterday, with Nancy's help, I was able to finally accept Debbie's crossing.

My minister's comment the following Sunday tickled me. Evelyn had said, "If you're going to walk on water, first you have to get out of the boat." So I got out of the boat.

Twenty-Eight:
All Hell's Breakin' Loose

Casey was putting more and more of his weight on his back leg now. He was eating good, getting up on the sofa, his favorite nap place, and jumping up on my bed was not a problem, although he seemed to think about it a little before he made the leap. Pat Silver was throwing another party. I talked to Allan, who is the artistic director for Express Theater, and he asked me if I could help him put together a reading series for "Express At Night". The reading would consist of standard favorite plays and new works. He also said that Express wanted to apply to the Dramatist Guild of American for membership and, since I was a member, could I provide information for them. And he said he wanted to open Express Theatre to me for any of my new plays and would I consider writing some children's plays for them that could be offered at the theater and also taken on the road to schools. Would I? They wanted adaptations of fairy tales with simple sets that would pack in the van. Talk about opportunity. Thank you, God.

That same week I received an invitation to enter *Show-Off*, a short play contest in Capistrano, California. That night I saw Eric Steel's documentary, "The Bridge" and was intrigued. In 2004, Eric filmed twenty-three people committing suicide jumping from the Golden Gate Bridge. Few survived. One was a young man who said he knew as soon as his fingers left the rail he wanted to live. On the way down he positioned himself so that he entered the water vertically. He really busted himself up but was conscious when he reached the surface. He said he felt something by his side and it was a seal. It nudged him and he hung on to it. The seal kept him afloat until help arrived. I was hooked. I wrote *JUMPER* in two days and sent it into competition. It won best play.

***

I was right. The Frenetic Theater would not be finished in time for the Fringe Festival and the whole deal had to be moved to Theatre Lab. A summer lease for the Lab was great news as they were going to be down most of that summer. All the props and costumes had to be transferred and it was raining like hell the day of the move. *Storm a-comin'*. Good thing Paul had a truck. He and I got the props to the door of the rehearsal hall and it suddenly quit raining just as one of our actors pulled up and helped us move everything. We had a two-hour rehearsal of *Nixon's Women* when we returned. I was running lines with the cast every day now. The show was scheduled to open August 30th, one week away.

Archway Readers called and asked if I would read from my book. How did that get out? Opportunity? Okay, okay, I get it. There are angels in my house today, very close.

On Saturday, the 23rd, I returned calls and read lines with Paul. His summer school classes were coming to an end but he was facing finals for his students, providing the finishing touches on *Nixon's Women* as star and director, had another play in rehearsal for Houston Community College's Theater One, holding down a part time job at Pottery Barn, and worrying about Katherine's recovery. He was stretched a little thin. I was giddy.

With all this activity, I was neglecting my spirituality and feeling distanced. My journal entries were short, prayer and meditation rushed, my colors seem faded, washed out. One morning I turned off the TV and got very quiet. Meditation came quickly. It usually did, but lately it had taken concentration every day. Colors appeared, primarily gold and blue. Huge swirling clouds, the biggest ever. I stayed in meditation for what seemed a long time watching them, looking inside them, and just resting. Then a firm voice, *"get off sugar and walk."* I came up and felt renewed, peaceful and joyous. I was ready to hit it again.

Katherine, Paul, Mom, and I decided we'd go in together for a beach house in Galveston for Thanksgiving week. God only knew what that would cost but we deserved it. The problem was finding one that would take dogs, our Duke and Casey, and Paul and Katherine's Roscoe, who gets up on the table to steal tidbits off your plate, and sweet little Puddin', who pees when you pet her. Just us and the dogs, we decided. No open house for theater folks, just us pigging out, sprawling on the deck, guzzling wine, and relaxing.

***

Hurricane Gustav was predicted to come calling the next week. We're too busy for a hurricane. I was running lines with Paul, doing rewrites, prayer, meditation, my thank you list, angel cards, the book, and every time the rainbow appeared on my study carpet there was a "Hi, Debs."

Gustav headed on down the coast and *Nixon's Woman* opened. It was a stunner. The audience was still applauding as the set was being struck for the next show. It was glorious, everyone congratulating Paul and cast after the show, Katherine and I ecstatic and jumping around outside on the sidewalk with cast members running into each other. There's nothing like this; it's better than sex. Then, the following night, came the final performance and that, my friends, was live theater. About ten minutes into the performance, Brenda threw Paul a line that was further along in the play and Paul went brain dead and blew out. They ran in circles for a few minutes trying to get back on line while the audience sat there astonished. Obviously, something was very wrong. Then our little Angelia Bracken, who played Nixon's secretary, Rose Mary Woods, you remember her, the tape lady, well, she called out a line that brought everybody back into this world and they brought it to an end. It wasn't that bad really, but the cast was devastated. Paul looked like he'd eaten bad oysters and all assumed the author would be suicidal, but I stayed calm and told them, "Look, guys, this happens in theater and we're just going to go on and prepare for next year's performance at Theatre One and not beat each other's brains out over it." Imagine Paul Young falling on his ass. What a leveler. Someday, he'll get quiet with his angels.

Sunday, September 7th, Mom and I drove to Galveston and found the beach house. Its decks reached to about fifty feet from the surf. It was old, beach beaten, had an outside shower, and lots of deck furniture. I took pictures of it, looked in windows, and drove back to Houston on top of the world. The following week, I called the number posted on the house. The owner wanted eight hundred for the week and no problem with the dogs. I don't think I specified four. The place wasn't The Ritz, but it was perfect for us. The owner lived in Liberty, Texas, and, after talking to her on the phone I felt there were some marital problems there, but they were not my problems, I just wanted to rent her beach house for an off-season week. She was thrilled to get the money. I called Paul and told him about it and he said, "Go." I wrote a check for four hundred dollars and threw it on my desk to be mailed to her the next day. *There's something brewing in the Gulf.*

I had a dream. Annie Forest, an old friend and coworker, had died and we were at her house. People coming to the funeral were out in the yard digging up her flowers and hauling them off. Mom was hauling with the best of them. I woke up. I hadn't heard from Annie in a long time, and knew she was not in the best of health. Some people just get lost in your life. I felt she'd passed and had sent me some of her energy in a dream.

There was another storm, Ike, heading for Corpus. *Hold on to that check.* Mom and I had lunch on the porch that day and I ordered *Life After Death* by Moody and *Healing Grief* by James Van Praagh from Amazon.com. It was a good day.

Monday, August 8th I went to a Scriptwriter's meeting as my mentor, Howard Paulson, as Director of Drama at St. Thomas University, was speaking and then went out to eat with old friends. I shoveled in tacos, drank some beer, and, God, it was great seeing everyone and shooting theater crap with them.

All eyes were on the Gulf.

Tuesday night I went to Compassionate Friends. A mother told of her twenty-six year old son who was a hit and run on I-10. He died at the hospital. Two years later, his twenty-two year old brother went to a party at a friend's house. He became sick and left for home. On the way he died of alcohol poisoning. He wasn't found until morning.

A father, practically held up, told of his twenty-three year old son's suicide. He was dazed and unbelieving.

A twenty-two year old student at Sam Houston State University was into everything the school had to offer. His grades were excellent, he excelled in drama, was on the debate team, but he had a blood sugar problem which he ignored. He was always arguing with his parents when they nagged, "test your sugar, eat right, and don't forget your insulin." One evening he called his mom just before he went out on a date and said he didn't feel so hot but was going anyway. During the evening he became very sick in the car and his date just left him there and walked back to her dorm. He spent the night in the car, alone, in a store parking lot. He was found in the morning by an employee who went to check out the lone car parked in the lot and called 911. That was at eight a.m. He died at nine-ten a.m. after a sugar coma. His worried mother had begun to check hospitals and finally found him. She was a single mom and he was her only child. The doctor came in and said, "He's dead. There was nothing we could do." Then he left the room. She stayed there alone until they came and found her some time later, on the floor.

A father told of his eighteen year old son who lived through brain and heart surgery as a baby only to die in a car accident the month before.

It was a joyous time, a California summer vacation for second-time newlyweds. Both had teenagers. He, a girl and she, a boy, and they were all headed for a large family reunion in San Diego. They had a great time. The kids were up all night talking, dancing, giggling, and swimming in the pool with young friends and family. Four of them, this couple's kids included, loaded into a car after deciding to go out for breakfast. All four fell asleep and the driver ran the car into a street light. The car blew up and all died in the fire. They flew home with their kids in closed caskets in the baggage compartment. This couple cried in each other's arms.

Then a late arrival made the scene—and a scene it was. She looked so haggard my first thought was "new loss." She sat down and the meeting monitor introduced her to the group, which was unusual. She was more than distraught. Five years ago her dad had died, the next year her oldest son was killed in an auto accident. The next year her daughter committed suicide over the loss of her brother. Then last January, she was diagnosed with cancer. Last month, her only surviving son's father died. She was having a terrible time with the boy, who was crazy with grief, and she was trying to hold them both together. "I came for help," she said, simply. There were two health care employees at the meeting and they jumped in suggesting solutions and a lawyer. "He's harmful to himself and to others," one said. "He'll be able to get treatment in a hospital or facility."

When it was my turn to speak I told about how hard it still was to go to the grocery store, to answer the phone, hoping it will be Debbie, and trying to find some good in all this. Then I heard that the second and third years were the hardest. That you've prepared yourself for the first birthday, holiday season, Mother's Day, all those firsts, but the second year you fall under the truck. I talked about the physical pain and my search for relief. I remembered the mother who said that she instinctively knew that if it had been she who passed and not her daughter; her daughter would not have survived such the loss. She knew she was the stronger one.

I heard talk about kindness that was found. A woman who was allowed to view her dead son and the night nurse who kept the funeral home people away until she was ready—eight and a half hours later.

I heard how many cannot clean out a passed loved one's rooms or sell vehicles. One woman had the wreck that her boy was killed in hauled home and just sat in it. There were parents who spent days and sometimes all night at gravesites. And then, suddenly, one mother will get it and say, "I can't wait to see her again."

It was unreal and I came home feeling almost lucky. God bless those at that meeting. The suffering in that room was beyond belief, but it was important for me to be there and to hear their stories, important that I not feel alone, that I had people around me who knew exactly how I felt, what I was suffering, and the loneliness I would continue to feel every day from then on.

Am I afraid to die? Not anymore, although the way I might go bothers me. We're so hung up on our bodies, always concerned about our weight, make-up, and the right clothes for the right occasion. And the men: what tie is best, will I go bald, is my penis too small, and what will happen when I can't get it up any more? Bodies are so secondary. A God-given casing we're to take care of but which will eventually fail us. Everything else goes on to heaven. If we only use a small portion of our brain here on earth, what's the rest for? I still have a lot of questions and a lot to learn. Thank you, God, for letting me see that Debbie's body, my body, and Mom's body are what we have and not who we are.

Twenty-Nine: Ike

Thursday, August 11th, I was sitting on my ass looking at the beach house deposit check lying on my desk. It would never be mailed.

I'd prepared all I could, cashed a check, bought food, dog food, batteries, extra ice, filled the gas tank and bathtub, got out the portable radio and flashlights, laid out candles and matches and whatever else I could think of. Hell, I'd been through hurricanes before. Ike was going to be a piece of cake.

The grocery stores were emptying out fast. Outside, I took down all the hanging pots and put them close to the house, then stripped the porch and stored all that stuff in the garage. I dismantled Debbie's memorial garden and shoved plants in the dog house. My next door neighbor helped me move all the big pots and porch furniture.

It was in God's hands now, but still I worried about my beloved porch, afraid a limb would be torn from the pear tree or a flying object would go sailing through the screens. How I loved having coffee and reading my paper out there in the cool of the morning, watching the pink horizon change to purple just before the sun came up over the pear tree. I thanked God for his protection and for my Hartford homeowners and Farmers flood insurance policies.

I watched the news late into the night, tracking the storm through Galveston and as it moved up I-45 heading for Houston. I dozed off and then suddenly awoke. The electricity was off and banshees were loose in the yard. I lit a couple candles, especially for Mom in her bathroom, and kept the flashlights close by and the radio on, not only for information but for comfort, a person's voice there in the dark while outside it sounded like the world was coming to an end.

In the morning, I checked the porch with my heart in my mouth, but all was well. The fence was still up and, although there were roof shingles scattered about the backyard, everything looked pretty good. Then I went out in the front yard and looked at the roof from that angle. Shingles, in many places, had been stripped down to the wood, and when I opened the garage door I saw about a quarter of the garage ceiling had fallen in from the water coming in through the hole in the roof. Roof bracings were split and the roof sagged where the shingles had been blown off. Branches, twigs, and leaves were everywhere. As the neighbors came outside to check their own damage we were grateful there was no flooding in our neighborhood. There was lots of wind damage but our homes were not under water. Most of Houston and the surrounding areas had been hit even harder. Some neighborhoods were floating.

Because I had a gas stove and water heater I could at least cook and take a shower. Cell phones were out, but I did contact my insurance company in Dallas on my land line and they told me to get the roof repaired quickly so there would be no more water damage inside. Adjusters would be in Houston Monday or Tuesday to settle claims. I called Pam in Tomball, and they were headed for a shelter. Their mobile homes had not fared well.

It rained all that morning and, of course, more water damage was done inside the house. I started to see water marks on the ceilings of Mom's room, her closet, her bathroom, and in my study. Houston was completely down. No power. The only good thing was that we had been told to "hunker down" and stay in place, so there were no freeway problems trying to evacuate millions of people. Houston had learned a hard lesson from Hurricane Rita.

Saturday and Sunday, the city began to stir. Grocery stores, running on generators, began to open a few hours a day, but ice was impossible to get. I still had the three bags I'd made in the freezer but they were melting fast. I transferred the ice to coolers and stored what I could cook from the freezer in them. Sunday was a pretty day and, wonder of wonders, a cool front blew in, dropping the temperature. It was quite pleasant. After putting everything to order on the porch, Mom and I camped out there most of the following days. She was very quiet and cooperative.

Neighbors began moving food and water to other neighbors who were without. If someone located ice they bought the limit and brought it back for folks who had none. People with generators made ice for others.

Monday the insurance adjuster called. He would be here Wednesday. I cleaned up the yard and garage as much as I could. Tuesday, FEMA PODS opened up, giving out food and ice. The lines were around blocks. You had to be in your car to be loaded up and that meant burning gas. There were absolutely no walk-ups. You had to have power to pump gas. Generators again.

Tuesday I found a company that sent out two workers who temporarily repaired the roof for five hundred dollars. By Wednesday, the food in the fridge was not safe and out it went. I cleaned it and kept the door open. Now we were running on two small coolers, but the Food Fair close to me was open and I had money, so I left the PODS to those who were in worse shape than we were. I also found two bags of ice early the next morning. One bag per family was all that was allowed, so I dragged mother down to the store so we could get two, one for each cooler. They had a big ice making machine at Food Fair. I asked them if, when they closed down at seven p.m., "Will the ice machine continue to make ice all night at three bags an hour." The answer was, "yes" so we were there at seven a.m. every morning when the store opened for our two bags of ice.

We managed. I offered showers and food to the neighbors as grills fired up along the street. We needed lots of prayer and patience.

Repairmen were coming in from all over the country to help get the power on. On Wednesday only thirty-three percent of the power had been restored. Downed trees thrown across power lines were the biggest problem. Gasoline was still hard to get, but there were a few stations open, running on generators.

We were okay. The water pressure was coming up fast. That meant you didn't have to fill the toilet by hand to flush it. I tried to stop Mom from running out into the yard to pee. I had to discourage that for weeks after the storm.

By Thursday, the grocery stores were being restocked but I-45 to Galveston was closed. Galveston was in bad shape. There were over twenty-thousand people in shelters; and Bolivar Island was no more. Agencies were trying their best to save animals and pets.

It was September 18th—Debbie's birthday. I'd promised her a big party for her fifty-second birthday. Mom and I had scrambled eggs and sausage on the porch. At night I burned carefully watched candles, but it was light until nine or so they didn't burn long. The radio was on day and night. The cool front soon passed and the humidity and temperature were climbing fast. Still there were one million homes without power.

On Friday, September 19th Mom and I were out on the porch. The Chicken Shack was open and I had just returned from a run to bring some home. It was about four in the afternoon when Mom said, "Did you know the light is on in the refrigerator?" I flew inside the house. One week in the heat, in the dark, and now—we had power. Thank you, Jesus!

When I walked the dogs the next morning I felt a tightening in my chest and a sort of burning sensation. Felt like heartburn. I said aloud, "Now what in hell's the matter with me?"

Thirty: Heartbreak

Things were still very serious in Houston and along the Gulf Coast. Power was beginning to be restored but slowly and sporadically. One whole block would get power back—all but three houses. Then extension cords would run from house to house and across streets to get a fridge back on, neighbors looking out for neighbors. There was still food, ice, and water at some FEMA PODS but they were beginning to run out and were not being restocked as planned. Families ran out of food, ran out of water, and were in the dark.

While walking the dog that next morning I again felt the tightening in my chest and my breath was coming hard. It still felt like heartburn so I went home, popped a few antacids, and sat down until it passed. For the next few days I was very careful what I ate and blamed the whole thing on stress, heat, anxiety, and Ike. I was getting estimates for a new roof and repairs for the garage. This was not the time for indigestion. Half the city was still down, gas was hard to find, and traffic lights were out. Who would care for Mom and the dogs if I had something serious wrong with me? Dr. Cleaver had been flooded and he was moving to a new office on the fourth floor. All these things were running through my mind. I've always been so proud of my healthy body. It couldn't let me down now. I put a lot of prayer into these things but my angel cards kept coming up, "heart chakra." Wasn't that terrific? As the days passed, the pressure eased up, although I still had spells of light-headedness, almost a dizzy feeling. My breathing was not so labored, but I was one very tired lady. I kept busy doing piles of laundry that had accumulated during the power outage and making Jezebel Sauce, a spicy glaze and dipping sauce. Ten jars for friends and two for me. What was I doing?

A welcomed cool front blew in at last. It was happy days until I fell into our large city garbage can and cut my lip and scraped my knee. Now, it is no easy thing to fall into a garbage can, but the lid was open and as I was bringing it in from the street I tripped and went in head first. Good thing it was dark, because I must have looked a sight, but was laughing as I picked myself up, went inside, and headed for Band-aids. No doubt about it Debbie, would have wet her pants.

The next day, Friday, October 25th, I had to take Mom and myself for flu shots.

We had an early morning appointment and after giving us the shots, Dr. Cleaver, asked how I was doing. "Well, I've got this heartburn thing going on," I answered him.

He looked at me over his glasses, asked me a few questions, ran an EKG and gave me the name of a cardiologist. He also gave me a prescription for Zoloft. I made an appointment for the treadmill thing and other tests and told myself to stay quiet.

Did I stay quiet? A stone got more exercise. Monday was September 29th. Debbie had passed eleven months ago. I had one small attack and was taking my "little friends" faithfully, three times a day. I was trying hard to give this whole mess to God and my angels and I sincerely asked for their help as I filed for FEMA, paid bills, and continued getting estimates for the new roof and ceiling repairs for the garage. I didn't think angels were in the repair business, but I knew they could send me in the right direction.

When I went to church Sunday I whispered to my pastor, "I'm in trouble." She took me aside and I told her that I might need someplace for mom to stay for a few days while I had this "heartburn" thing looked into. The procedure, if needed, seemed simple enough. Go in as an outpatient, they would give me a happy pill and run a line to my heart to find the blockage, then pop in a stent to inflate the artery and I go home the next day. On Tuesday, Janice, Evelyn's assistant, called from the church and told me she'd take Mom—and me as well if the need arose. Thank you, God, and all my angels.

I've got a couple of angels living next door to me who check on me regularly, Jack and Wanda Petri. We've been neighbors for about twenty-five years. I've watched their kids grow up and they were with me every step of the way with Debbie. So I called and told them what was going on and they said they'd run over and feed the dogs if I had to have any kind of procedure and see that everything was okay.

The Petri's had a problem and his name was Charlie. Charlie was a seven month old black lab puppy who'd moved into their home at the same time their daughter, Beth, and granddaughter, Mickey, did. Beth had made the painful decision to divorce her husband of one year. I didn't ask. Anyway, Andy, their son, was getting married the following Saturday. Big wedding, all day job. And what to do with Charlie, who was, I gathered, digging holes in their backyard so big you could bury fire stations in them? Now, I had a great dog house in my backyard that I didn't use anymore, and ever since I had the porch built, Casey and Duke relaxed in the lap of luxury out there with rugs, fans, and a dog door. I gave Beth the dog house and told her I'd look out for Charlie. Problem solved. We are all loved, safe, and protected.

I was cutting down on the Zoloft now and feeling pretty good. Maybe it was just stress, eating the wrong things, taking care of Mom, and this Ike thing. Probably wasn't a blockage at all. Then I hit on acid reflux. That sounded good to me. I sometimes had a slight stirring in my chest but it went away when I sat down and one day I just walked it off in the grocery store. Killing time, I was doing a lot of fun reading, *Lincoln* by Vidal, another *Lincoln* by Donald. They were both second readings.

By October 3rd I was off the anxiety pills and keeping it together. I just couldn't be zonked out of my mind and take care of Mom. That night I had a dream. I was in the hospital in a double room. Mom was standing close to the bed and Debbie was on the other one, chattering away. I don't remember what she was saying but I remember thinking how wonderful for her to be there yakking away and laughing with me like old times. Then I thought, she's really here and this other stuff has gone away. I woke up to the reality that this was only a dream, Debbie had really died, and I might have a problem. It was three a.m. I thanked God for the visitation—and knew that I would be going to the hospital and she would be there with me.

I went to get a new license plate and sticker for the car that next morning. There was still the tightness in my chest but no attacks. I was dreaming a lot of past junk, and I mean junk. There were ex-husbands, moving all over the country, old friends having an affair with my husband. When I woke up I just called on my angels and asked God to get rid of all that garbage so I could go on. That was another person.

I was still working on getting a roofer, me and about two million other people in Houston; out of seven calls, I received two replies for an estimate. Finding a roofer in Houston right then was a miracle. Ron, the guy who painted my house four years earlier, was coming to fix the ceiling in the garage, and secure the cracked 8x10's holding up the roof. The economy was blowing out and my investments were folding along with everyone else's. There was certainly a lot going on to keep my angels busy. I was having a hard time coping with it all, but was staying off the pills and hanging in there. I was going to be okay.

One of my roof estimators seemed to be an honest, hard-working sort of guy so I called his references and he checked out. I talked to a minister who had this guy put roofs on his church and home. "He's the best," I was told, and he got my business. Thank you, God.

I'd been asked to read at Archway Readers and I rewrote the preface of the book I'd been working on as my offering that night. I had an attack that morning while walking the dogs. I had to come on home and pop a pill. It was October 10th and I was to go for tests on the 15th. I hoped I'd make it. God Bless HMO's. I'd just gone over the expenses to fix Ike's damage to the house: the roof, the new ceiling, painting, and my microwave oven had blown up. But with the insurance check and with mine and Mom's Social Security checks that month I might just be able to squeeze through without going into savings. We did. My angels were amazing.

The reading went well. Better than I expected. The audience was with me all the way and at the break asked all the right questions. Do you really believe in angels? Where do you really go when you go to heaven? Will my dog go to heaven? How do I meditate? Not being an expert, I tried to answer as honestly as I could. I had a couple of bubble ups when Debbie was mentioned, but I got through it.

Monday, October 13th the roof was on and it looked good. I only had one attack that morning and it passed quickly.

The Christmas play at the church would be done December 14th.

Paul called to tell me he's leaving me six tickets for Mom, me, and friends to see his adaptation of Romeo and Juliet at Theater One.

I was getting ready for the tests and maybe a procedure by taking the dogs to get their nails clipped, and stocking up on dog food and frozen dinners. Then I gave my furry friends a bath. They ignored me the rest of the day.

By Wednesday, September 15th I was ready. It meant four hours in Dr. Verdun's office on and off the treadmill while wired up. I felt like an astronaut. "I'll call you later with the results," he told me, and I went home to wait it out. He called. One of my heart's arteries was blocked. It meant angioplasty, but it didn't require anesthetic so it was just a 24-hour stay in the hospital. The procedure was admittance in the a.m. one day and out in the a.m. the next day. I could handle that. I asked God to send his angels to help me and I asked those same angels to get me through this. I needed a lot of help: Michael for strength, Raphael for healing, Gabriel for protection, Uriel for providing answers through his step-by-step method of solving all problems, Azriel to just kind of hang around in case I needed him.

There was a lot to do yet. I needed a ride to and from the hospital. Dorothy, who would take care of Mom, handled that. Beth, next door, would watch and feed the dogs, who were to be kept on the porch. We were moving along. I am loved, protected and safe, and all will be provided.

Was I surprised at the diagnosis? Nope. I could feel something was wrong. I just put myself and all the problems in God's hands and knew they would be resolved. This was a learning experience for me. Give it away. And it all started with the oranges. It's not the problems; it's how I handle them. Even better, it's how I don't handle them and let them go. I let God and my angels take the whole mess and got myself out of the way. I was trying hard to embrace my future positively. Thank you, God, for my blessings, my church, my friends, my mom, my dogs and my angels.

I was scheduled for October 22nd. Everything was in place. Repairs done, Paul had all the information he needed to take care of things. On October 20th I went in for pre-op and who was my nurse? Bridgett, the lady who runs the bookstore at my church. Was I ever glad to see her, because, quite frankly, I was scared out of my gourd and I told her as much.

"Don't be afraid," she replied. "I'm going to be looking in on you and Evelyn and Dorothy are coming. There's going to be so many people in that room there won't be space for the doctor. We do many of these procedures every day and you're going to be fine. This is a quick fix."

Yeah, I thought. Sure.

Thirty-One: A Quick Fix

Dorothy picked us up right on time and we were at the hospital at seven a.m. She and Mom drove off as I entered the hospital, but I wasn't alone. Man, I had a crowd of angels with me. Before I knew it I was on the table and given my "happy pill" and the crew went to work inserting the wires through my arm and into my heart. I felt nothing and could see and hear everything that was going on as I happily drifted in and out on my pink cloud. Man, the room was like a laboratory. There were machines and hook-ups all over the place. There was even what looked like a sound booth on my right side. They worked for what seemed a long time. Finally, I heard the magic words, "Okay, we're done."

"Is it over?" I asked.

"Yep, sure is, but we had problems. Your artery is so small we couldn't get the stent inserted. We tried several sizes—and quite a few times. We're going to send you upstairs and fix you up good tomorrow." What he was saying was open heart surgery.

I don't remember much else about that day or the next except that I had someone call Dorothy and Paul and Katherine, to tell them there was a monkey wrench in my machinery. What I do remember was someone saying, "Patricia? It's time to wake up." So I pushed myself into some sort of consciousness. My mouth was so dry it felt like a Sierra sand dune and I lay there very still, only moving my eyes.

Finally, I asked, "Could I please have some ice chips?" I was really thirsty. Within seconds it was there. I was in the ICU unit and would not be moved into a room. Before I could take in the room I drifted off into never-never land and that's when it happened. It felt like I could have been asleep but I instinctively knew I wasn't. The room felt very close and what I could see was a vastness beyond my understanding. There was no tunnel or bright light. I could see no one but I knew there was a presence there. I felt beings around me. Was it nurses, tech people? Who knew? I certainly didn't. I just knew that room was full of something. There was a pressure reminding me of what it was like in the car the night Debbie passed. It was misty, heavy, and it was right above me. I could have reached out and touched it. Then I heard my own voice.

"It's okay. Take me home now. I'd rather be with Debbie anyway but I'd better stay around because I have a lot of things to finish up here. There's taking care of Mom and the dogs, the book, and maybe a couple more plays, but it's up to you. I'm ready now if that's what you want."

And then, in answer, only one word: *"Stay."* And I was brought around again.

"Patricia, stay awake now, we have lots of things to do for you." It was the head nurse. "Please call me Pat. My mom calls me Patricia, but only when I'm in trouble." She was right, there was a lot to do and this was just the beginning of my way back.

They knocked me out for the rest of that day and night but tech people came and went all the time checking blood, temperature, blood pressure, blood sugar, feet, and what have you. "Are you in pain?" "Yes." "Okay, from one to ten." "Ten." Then someone would shoot something into a tube and off I would go again. In the morning I became aware of the room and the ton of equipment in it. There was hardly room for the nursing staff. They were crawling over stuff, moving this out of the way to make room for that.

The next day, Friday, October 24th, they had the audacity to make me get up, walk a little and then go to the bathroom. I wasn't one bit happy about all this as they had to unhook me from about twenty lines running from God knows what. I didn't want to do anything. The only thing I wanted was drugs!

They sent in a breakfast tray but all I could get down was a small portion of grits. I loaded them with sugar and milk and the few bites I took were wonderful but that was it. Dorothy and Evelyn came by, they later told me. "Was I there?" I asked Evelyn.

"Sure," she answered, "you were the one in the bed."

I couldn't eat, I couldn't shit, and they made me get up and pee on a portable pot or a bed pan. The only thing I knew for sure was that I was flat on my back, helpless, dependent, and hating it. I was at the bottom of the barrel. There was no backing out of this or fighting it. So I completely surrendered. There was only one place to go: to God and my angels. "If you want me out of here then let's get after this healing thing."

I asked Dorothy not to bring Mom in as I didn't want her frightened by all the equipment—not to mention, I must have looked pretty scary myself. But she gave Dorothy a hard time until she brought her in for a short time.

Dorothy told me she had found a caregiver service that would come to my home and take care of mom, me, and the dogs for two weeks as soon as I went home. Two weeks didn't sound like a very long time to me. It turned out to be an eternity.

Sunday, October 26th the routine didn't change except I had to walk down the hall with a walker, but, hey, the sponge baths were terrific. It seemed like there was a nurse in the room most of the time and they were stumbling over angels. Angels, who were helping me walk, eat ice cream, and go to the bathroom. It was an angel convention and the conversations between us never stopped. They talked directly to me through my mind and I talked to them. *"You're going home tomorrow."*

"I can't. That's only Monday. Four days is not enough time," I argued.

"It's enough time for us."

Monday I went home. Dorothy came and picked me up. Mom was in the car and Beth and Jack were at the house.

My caregivers were waiting for me and the dogs were bouncing like balls, they were so excited to see me. After a quick hello, it was a pain pill and sleep time, healing sleep. Dealing with my caregivers was hard for me. I was completely dependent on their care of me, Mom, and the dogs, and I knew it. I was sweet and cooperative, but deep down I hated every minute of it.

Beth arranged for her cleaning girl, my wonderful Alma Rodriguez, who came in once a week and my yard man, Anzo Morales, who continued every two weeks caring for my yard. Anzo, who, if I was out on the porch, turned off the mower and always took a few minutes to visit with Mom and me. Not that there was much left of the yard. It looked like a blow torch had been taken to it and all the plants were deader than door nails. Well, better them than me. I slept, took my pills, prayed, and thanked my angels for hanging around. It was October 29th —the one year anniversary of Debbie's passing. I missed it, drugged to the teeth.

For the next two weeks I was up and down. First, I'd get into my recliner for a while and then go back to bed. I had to ask myself every day, "Am I hurting?" "No." "Am I breathing?" "Yes." "Am I comfortable in bed?" "Yes." "Am I going to get through this day and night?" "Yes." "Am I going to have a bowel movement today?" "Questionable."

After the first week we developed a caregiver problem. After I fell asleep one afternoon, Sarah just left. It was maybe four o'clock in the afternoon. She'd left us something to eat but was gone. I was in no shape to take care of myself or Mom. I got mad considering that I was paying out the nose for this service and we had a talk the next day. She told me her kids called with a problem at home and she had to leave early. My answer, "That's your problem. Mine is here, and I need you to do your job."

I'm back.

My home bound physical therapy started with exercises. I could hardly lift my arms or legs I was so weak. I kept doing them. Paul and Katherine came by for a short visit but I was really too tired for company. Mom kept coming into my bedroom, petting me, and asking if I was okay. "Sure," I'd answer her. Satisfied, she would then paddle off to bed. I had no idea what she was aware of, but, no doubt about it, I was hurting and I was scared. My greatest fear was what would happen to Mom and the dogs if I died. Who would take care of them? It was a lot to turn over to overworked angels.

For the next few days I watched the news and Cash Cab to see if I'd lost any of my mental capabilities. I had, but they were coming back. Monday, November 3rd and Obama's grandmother had passed. It was the day before the election but I knew after the votes were counted she'd be well aware of our new president. Dee-Dee, my African-American caregiver, was beside herself. She was so excited she left a can of soda in the freezer and it blew up in the middle of the night. She remembered it a few blocks from the house but, what the hell, she went on home anyway. What I mess. I took one look and closed the freezer door. This was getting old and my patience running thin. Angel talk, *"Get up."* And I got up for good. I'm going to fight this through, I thought. With God's help all this will soon pass.

I reminded Dee-Dee the next day was garbage pickup and asked her to take the can to the curb. She forgot and Mom and I struggled to get it out there. She told me when she remembered it she was around the corner from the house. Did it occur to her to come back and do her job? Hello.

Physical therapy continued and now I was walking two houses every morning. I was sleeping on my left side because my ribs were so sore on the right I couldn't stand the pressure. But I was healing, showering, washing my hair, and managing again. It just felt like I had a hockey puck in my chest. But now I had goals: walk and, holy of holies, drive to Paul and Katherine's house for a gourmet Thanksgiving dinner. I'd lost twelve pounds. That was a good thing.

By November 11th we were on our own. Sarah drove me to the surgeon and he released me to Dr. Wyn, my cardiologist. Dee-Dee, Sarah, their inattention, and the daily retelling of their life histories were gone from my life. The surgeon said I could drive in a week. I drove to the store the next day with a throw pillow between me and the steering wheel. I kept seeing "feathery" beings in my peripheral vision and had a feeling of peace, knowing all would be well. Beth stayed with Mom and I drove to my appointment with Dr. Wyn. He released me for three months.

Neighbors were bringing in food but I still had no appetite. My sternum was healing, but slowly. I was just taking it easy and letting my angels take care of everything. I concentrated on breathing, walking, paying bills, and driving to the store and bank. That was it for me. I slept a lot, and, thank God, so did Mom.

Thanksgiving Day arrived and I drove us to the pay-off dinner. I ate very little and was a bit shaky. We left early but it was great to be out again. Besides, I had angels to lean on.

The day after Thanksgiving, I went back to the computer and my book.

***

Do I still have "bubble ups" when I think of Debbie? You bet. Do I worry about my health? Sure. Is the economy sending me to the nut house? Of course. Am I concerned about Mother? Every day. Good thing I don't have to handle these things by myself. I have my friends, my church, Compassionate Friends, the whole crew at Houston Hospice that will care for me, Mom, and I have angels, angels, angels.

# Let's Talk About Angels, Angels, Angels

I think when God created a hundred million angels for the express purpose of helping us out of our messes and being so generous that he gave each one of us one of our own to see us through, He had an even bigger plan in mind. That's a lot of angels, and I think he gathered his flocks and divided them up to do certain jobs. Otherwise, it would have been angel chaos and God doesn't work that way. So when we get ourselves into trouble or a frame of mind that calls for the expertise of a certain group of angels, there they are ready to help.

Our personal guardian angels are just that. They guard us constantly, are with us wherever we are, and are involved in whatever we're doing. Have you ever had a harrowing experience? Rest assured your guardian angel was there to haul you out. Pay attention to your intuition—that's your guardian angel nudging you. Did you ever have a "go" feeling regarding an idea or a "hold it" where you felt like you were being hauled in on a choke chain? Guess who? Pay attention! Sometimes something may happen to you that will convince you your guardian angel is in Barbados having an umbrella drink. How could this happen to me, you say? Where is God and my guardian angel? This angel garbage is a lot of bunk! Well, all I can say is that shit happens and when it does thank God for all my loving, comforting guardian angels. That's right, angels. You can have more than one, you know.

Have you ever been stumped? I mean flat out brain dead when it comes to a problem in your life? Then out of the blue pops up an answer. You can't imagine how you missed it. That's an angel's job: delivering messages and solving problems when you miss them.

Then you've got your backup angels. They're the ones behind you one hundred and ten percent with their *"You can do this. I'm here to help you all the way."* Or a *"Great job, I knew you could do it. Now let's try something else. You're ready and all you have to do is be willing."* Sometimes all I have to do is turn on the computer.

Second-in-command angels are ready to take over the bus when you give out. That's right. There they are doing everything that has to be done and, just between you and me, doing a better job of it. All you have to do is ask, turn it over to them, whisper a "thank you" and be on your way. What could be simpler?

Angels that come to us delivering messages either through meditation or dreams are our "comfort angels." Remember, angels can take on any form that suits them or the moment, but they won't do or say anything that would frighten you. If a full-fledged, eight foot, glowing, angel with six foot wings appeared in my kitchen, I wouldn't have to take my blood pressure pills or worry over a bowel movement any longer. These are the angels that comfort our grief, hold us, rock us, show us hope, feel our sorrow, and then take it on as their own.

The healing angels work on many fronts. Are you scared out of your mind with an illness? Are you harboring bitter feelings against someone? Did you lose a job you loved or even one you didn't? Did your spouse run off with the local beer rep? Did your parents pass on before you had a chance to say goodbye? Healing angels can fix all the many troubles of your life. Just pray to God to send his healing angels to you, tell them what you need, thank them for solving the problem *before* they go to work and just sit back and watch it happen.

Do you believe in coincidence? Not me. Not anymore. I believe in fast track angels—working it.

If a truck backed over me I'd be on the angel horn fast. "Please get me out of here and thanks for your time." Like a St. Bernard, one will arrive on cue. You just have to ask God to send one of his angel helpers.

If you have trouble asking just sit down and write a note to your angels.

Dear Angels:

I need you to take over the following because I'm just a mess and can't handle it. Thank you for taking all this on and resolving it to my higher good. (Pick some.)

Money-Health-Job/School-Car Repairs-New Car/Home Decision-In-Laws -Boyfriend/Husband-Parents-Anger/Fear

Thank you again, my angels, for the guidance and solutions you bring to me.

Sign Your Name

Date:

Put it in an envelope, address it to your angels, or specifically if you know who, Michael, Gabriel, Raphael, Uriel, Ariel, or Azriel. If you really want to have some fun stamp it, mail it, and see what happens.

One thing I know about angels they're not into gloom and doom. They're gracious, warm, happy, creatures that want nothing more than to instill these characteristics in you. They love to hear you laugh, enjoying a party with friends, delighting in a quiet dinner or a good book. Man, a good book and a peanut butter and jelly sandwich and look out! The only thing better is to haul the whole mess back to bed and pull the quilt up to my chin. Before long, the dogs will come to snuggle up. Good thing I have a king-size bed because they love company and peanut butter. Joy and laughter can defeat anxiety, fear, and sorrow in a heartbeat. Try it. There's a laughter angel right by your left shoulder.

Something More About Angels

In my research I'd read that the word "Angel" appears over three hundred times in the bible. Now, I don't know about three hundred times but while comparing Bible verses against various books on angels, *Heaven* by Randy Alcorn, *Spirit Guides and Angels* by Richard Webster, and *How to Meet and Work with Spirit Guides* by Ted Andrews, and many others, I found a ton of angels. Michael and Gabriel seem to have been kept pretty busy in both the Old and New Testaments from Genesis to Revelations. There are lots and lots of angels who seem to have been around for about ten thousand years. Angels were found pictured on the walls of tombs and figurines were unearthed resembling our concept of angels as far back as 2500 BC.

I think angels have been around since before creation. Maybe God was lonesome and created angels to keep him company in heaven. Maybe it didn't help his loneliness so he created the universe, including our earth, mankind, and all the animals, birds, and everything else he could think of that would be sort of fun to mess around with. But, not so good, not enough one-on-one, so Adam and Eve were created and God saw it was all pretty cool. But some of the angels really got pissed including one sorry excuse for an angel, named Satan. They weren't about to take a back seat to all this creation stuff so they pulled out and Satan did a job on Adam and Eve in the Garden of Eden with the tree and the snake thing. God was furious and threw Adam and Eve out of the garden but where to put these renegade angels? Hell would be a good place, and so it was.

Now, although one-third of God's angels lived in this new place with the good heating system, God had lots of angels left over and they all lived together happily in heaven. But God and his angels kept a keen eye on earth and His querulous humans. He sent his angels back to earth frequently to check up and report to Him what was going on down here. So angels have been visiting earth since the beginning of time.

Angels are neither male nor female and can take any form depending on their mission. Angels are kept pretty busy but if you feel the need for an angel, only ask God to send some to meet your needs and they'll be on their way.

God created so many angels that he was able to give each human his very own guardian angel. Hard cases got more than one in addition to the angels who were already delivering His messages between heaven and earth.

Do we become angels when we die? Sorry, God created lots of angels and the number has not increased or decreased since that time and they're very good at following orders. We don't pray to angels, we pray to God, and He sends these wonderful beings to us on earth to guard us, fight for us, counsel us, be with us when we're born and escort us to heaven when we die. Angels have their own back stories, their own personalities, memories, jobs, colors and names. No one knows us better than the angels, except God.

There are nine groups of angels and they have their own celestial hierarchy. These groups are divided into three categories or triads.

<u>FIRST TRIAD – IN THE PRESENSE OF GOD</u>

Seraphim – These angels stay in the presence of God and never come to earth.

Cherubim – Provide protection and knowledge. They guard the stars and the Tree of   Life.

Thrones – God's transportation system – they transfer energy to us through our Guardian Angels.

<u>SECOND TRIAD – ORGANIZING AND MINISTERING</u>

Dominions – Make sure every angel is utilized.

Virtues – Provide strength and courage.

Powers – Protect heaven – they are the warrior angels.

<u>THIRD TRIAD – MOST INVOLVED WITH EARTH</u>

Principalities – Look after earthly continents, nations, and cities and continually transfer information between heaven and earth.

Archangels – God's important messengers. Each has a name.

Angels – Assigned to individuals, work with all other angels. When help is needed any angel can request it from any other angel or God.

Now, I'm not going to cloud the angel issue with the millions of angels that God has created or the lengthy list of Archangels that I deal with daily with my angel cards. I'm just going to tell you about my "Big Five" – Michael, Gabriel, Raphael, Uriel, and Azreal.

<u>MICHAEL: (HE WHO IS LIKE GOD)</u> – The Warrior – Color: Red or Royal Blue. Michael is with you at all times and protects you from evil. He will relieve your fears while providing a feeling of safety. He stopped Abraham from sacrificing his son Isaac (Gen 22:10), appeared to Moses in the burning bush (Exod 3:2), rescued Daniel from the lion's den (Dan 6:22), and is believed to have advised Joan of Arc. I call upon Michael if I feel myself in danger or feel I need strength in a situation. Michael will lead Christ's angels in the final battle between good and evil. When I need a champion, I want Michael on my side.

<u>GABRIEL: (GOD IS MY STRENGTH)</u> – Truly God's Messenger: Color: Emerald/Sea Green - Sits at the left hand of God and is the second most important Archangel. Gabriel has a connection to births as he was the angel that visited Zacharias and told him his wife, Elizabeth, would mother John the Baptist (Luke 1:11-20). It was Gabriel who told Mary she

was to give birth to Christ (Luke 1:26-27), and informed Daniel of the coming of the Messiah (Dan 9:21-27). Gabriel is very interested in creative writing, leadership, protection, and nurturing our inner child. Gabriel is mostly pictured as female but can appear in many forms.

RAPHAEL: (SHINING ONE WHO HEALS) Color: Blue – Raphael is the healing Archangel and the third most important. He is believed to have healed the wounds of martyrs and protects travelers. Raphael awakens a sense of creativity and beauty. Whenever you are in need of healing whether it is physical or spiritual, Raphael is the one to call on as his dark blue aura will help remove your concerns and bring you into perfect alignment with your health and happiness. I believe Raphael to be my Guardian Angel.

URIEL (THE FIRE OF GOD) Color: Pale Yellow—Uriel is the Archangel of creative ideas. He provides intellectual guidance, as well as creative insights. Through repetitive thoughts he will provide answers in a step-by-step approach to solving a problem. Pay attention to your thoughts and ideas, they are answered prayers. He employs a claircognizance approach to your problems and if you ask him for help an answer will pop into your head in an instant.

AZREAL (WHOM GOD HELPS) Color: Vanilla Cream. Now this is an Archangel who's gotten a bum rap. Known as the Angel of Death, he is far from the dismal and scary creature this title would imply. Instead, Azreal helps us deal with grief. He sits with us, holds us, lifts us from the dark hole of loss and stays with us until we can breathe on our own again. He says he is with us in our time of need helping your heart to heal. He assists our loved ones in crossing over and escorts them to the gates of heaven where they are met by family and friends and brings us messages from deceased loved ones. He advises grief counselors and helpers and assists loved ones in making contact. He would even go so far as to activate a turn signal on an automobile just to prove a point.

So these are my personal five angels but there are many more: Jeremiel, Zedekiel, Raziel, Jophiel, Haniel, Sandalphon, to name a few. They all have special jobs and will help you through whatever trouble comes your way. Read about them, get acquainted with them, and learn how each and every angel has your best interests at heart. They love you, as God does, and they help God help you.

***

In closing, just know that if your child passes, they are not just of your past; they are of your future.

For He will command his angels concerning
you to guard you in all your ways.
Psalm 91:11

THE BEGINNING

References

My Church: Unity Church of Christianity – Check your phone book or net.

My Support Group: Compassionate Friends – Check your phone book or net.

A Holistic Center: Ask around and you'll find a center near you that will open your world.

My Bookcase:

Out On A Limb - Shirley MacLaine

The Camino - Shirley MacLaine

Messengers of Light - Terry Lynn Taylor

One Last Time - John Edward

After Life - John Edward

Life After Life - Raymond A. Moody, Jr. M.D.

90 Minutes in Heaven - Don Piper

Questions from Earth-Answers from Heaven - Char Margolis

Healing Grief - James Van Praagh

Heaven - Randy Alcorn

How to Meet & Work With Spirit Guides - Ted Andrews

Hello From Heaven - Bill and Judy Guggenheim

Connecting With Your Angels Kit - Doreen Virtue, PhD

Angel Guidance Board - Doreen Virtue, PhD

Archangel Oracle Cards - Doreen Virtue, PhD

Daily Guidance From Your Angels - Doreen Virtue, PhD

About the Author

Pat came out of the glossies and started writing plays in 1986. After thirty productions nationwide she's still writing plays. Pat has won the Texas Women's Repertory Project Award, was a finalist in the Texas Playwright's Festival, is a CAACH grant recipient, won "best play" at the Camino Real Theatre's Show Off Competition in California and was presented at First Stage. Her full-length *Capote Tonight* opened in Houston at Express Theatre in May, 2007; *The Last Posse* opened at the Lodestar Theater, NYC, in April, 2007; and her ten-minute play, *Sex Games*, won the Scriptwriters/Houston 2007 first prize. She is published in both adult and children's plays, is a proud member of the Dramatist Guild of America, is a founding member of Scriptwriters/Houston, and is Playwright in Residence at Pasadena Little Theater. *Angel Tracks* is her first novel.

ALL THINGS THAT MATTER PRESS ™

FOR MORE INFORMATION ON TITLES AVAILABLE FROM
ALL THINGS THAT MATTER PRESS, GO TO
http://allthingsthatmatterpress.com
or contact us at
allthingsthatmatterpress@gmail.com

www.ingramcontent.com/pod-product-compliance
Lightning Source LLC
Chambersburg PA
CBHW071212260626
47162CB00004B/1264